[Ruptured] >> Schematic << MAZES

by
Joshua Martin

Some of these pieces were originally published
by   *experiential-experimental-literature,*
Nauseated Drive, Don't Submit!, Black Stone /
White Stone, SORTES, Streetcake, Beir Bua, and
The Vital Sparks

[Ruptured] >> Schematic << MAZES

turning dilemma raincoat eyelids
flowing manic forgetting paths
leading voices contemporary(kisses brave)<exile
                        waters over=turned>::
  burning strains perilous madmen
    dazing / overturned / inadequate cars(sleep)
upturned
        fl
        es
        h)[(like boneless)mistaken
                ident
                ity lingering
                brush fires desert promises
                    un
                lost]— loose
jamming=hammer= jilted to/for/over/under/
drenched in

distances
        screaming
                  f>o>r>w>a>r>d
stepped
    tap danced
        (beguiling gestures/
          move
            ments/
              orange ice cream
              roof of mouth
          stuck
          sticky
          residue
          co-

2

                    mingling)—

once blue moon harvest suntan crowbar to
smash car windshields onion smelling hands dry
skin neck crash course anarcho promises spread
wealth swallow the rich damn the elites create
function works diametrically opposed
parameters left/right/center nonsense ridiculing
rivals that require ridicule/ partakes river
running rooming house tirades drug addict
avarice corporate crimes crooks conspiracy
criminalize poverty throw stones bank windows
running stumbling

never=
      nowhere=
      not=
      nothing=
      non=
      none=
      no how=[(needless)(draped in
                  corn stalks)(grand
                  backwards,cracked,crumbl
                           ing)]— clouds of
obtuse hairpieces
hazy demeanor unpacks.spools of grease
hands a-plenty,shallow rails jumping ridden
indication ensues.here hounding variety a store
brand label advertisement
                        face tattoo
[(boo hoo)(boo)hoo]
all aboard all aboard
above/below/still buried
                        maybe

alive?
maybe
asleep?
may
            be
may
            be??????????

///

one question   to nostrils   ease breath
        tongues dancing   arms   stutter
            held in   wish to
day(s))...
[()()()()()()()()()...still stutter...()()()...oh
please...oh please...()()()()()...
at ease
        ...()()()()...
            oh please...
oh please...()()()]

breaking circumstances hollowed eyed tradition
like water infants aching hostile streaming
back to thee,will yield floor,bare dilemmas
spots,deliveries,again& again in-
                    crease or cease to
                    exist in formation
                    the foundation sink

                                    i

                                    n

                                    g

study callous bent position
boxes lending coherence
cease to render fades in feet

ears
    that twitch
    with earlobe<earthquakes>bisected office
building
drama curtain
      pulling/tugging rug
                      slip
not unlike a banana peel:::::::::::::
                          obviously subversion
""
"" "" (loafs
        a loafer
            loafing) watch hands hairy
                    if crisis/:::

(smoking joint
crippled army
headquarters
soldiers failed
draining like
cans of warm beer
likely barbaric
sickly broken spigots
dust bowl
machines ramble
on & on &
onward &on)

      theory dangling
      dysfunction
        stray,hairs,undertaking '' unrendered fat
'':::

              "pardon dandruff acquiescence
              of telephone graveyards

5

grasses green overgrown
bridges glimmer shimmer
lounge"/

fields   of   endless
edges

embodiment whistling teeth
old refrain:::seaweed:::to feed:::fire
spitting:::savage:::perpetual:::
pullllllllllllllllllllllllllllllllllllllllllllllll
unuttered hospital gown   slobs of
shoes   basics
                          anticipated
kingfishers   on the verge
     0f   ABCs,,,,,,,,,sustained
visions,,,,,,,,,,,,,,,,distances,,,,,,,,,,,,,
stray threads:
               the yarns!!!!!!! mistook planted
afloat??????????
…………   drifting
pits<age><of>=======bombs,,,,,,,,
     h0megr0wn apathy + rigor + stick that
sticks
catch as catch as might as swords as finch pinch
cinch wrench
d=i=t=c=h;;
;;;;;;;;;;;;;;;;;;;;;;;;;
>touch void stretching invisibility coldest
upends clutter pockets cheaply adorned
vocabularies that pertain to frown
back of hall constructed heads stuffed<cushions
precarious crumbs

couches colors flaw
          rug did bunch,ceased dramatic
horses,history a metal pole
weight of television monitors nightingale
twilight
gusts malfunction remotely freshly frequently
relics
sneezing demeanor/endeavor
flying remain mistook patches
collapsible expressions   .
costume moldy

                                        sky

shutters raid

deserted beads of
          >>>>freezing>>>>sweat<<<<
[ray of unlit (fire)crackers (post)industrial
disemboweled
manifestations array of stunning MyThS = = = =
evaporating luck
               plunge a beautiful embrace;;;
               climbing slightly h u n c h e d
                         :::
:::
    . token coughing trouble spittle course
highway loathes inconvenient
        peak a horror . soft a rest a head . a weary
. a horded brain .
country = = = = = = = = = = side = = = = = = = =
= = .

(back)lit emBRACE jacket POCKets
after<MATH>

,,,polymorphous lung decline,,,,unprepared response,,,provoke
engulf swwwwwaaaaaaaayyyyyyyyy,,,,aim an ideology,,,,steamoflength
HEAR[say] attention S   P   A   N
advvvvventuresssss ppplayed
in l o o o o o o o o o o o o o o ps,,,,,,,,discover zero intuition radiating
WHIPlash FLow BacK resi=due . muscles neck inch upWARDS . 1000s
promise(d) center w/0 yes . words LANGUAGE disappoints:::::speak:::::
carried choice   saNitY   center w/0 AN anCHor never filled
,,,,,,,capacity fading,,,,,,,,,,empty maneuvers [HIDDEN]causes – cave walls –
mass contemplation elation piano tuned to automatic<,,,>;;;< "" > handed
down finger temple gesture Rapid Fire slipping:

vague b/c

cheers

BoTTomS Up

steps to wet FLOOR unconsciousness
                              1st:LY varieties
                  2nd:LY perversions
                                       thirdLY carry the
1
thusly,opaque,
        therefore,preached .   miss
amiss be(ware)

                           stare instinctual

rotTING
hectic unfiltered ASSholes[unbleached!]against
greed W(a)<L>l[s]
wild at soil   open fire::::::

RAT=TAT=TAT=TAT RAT=TAT=TAT=TAT
RAT=TAT=TAT=TAT RAT=TAT=TAT=TAT
RAT=TAT=TAT=TAT RAT=TAT=TAT=TAT
RAT=TAT=TAT=TAT RAT=TAT=TAT=TAT
RAT=TAT=TAT=TAT RAT=TAT=TAT=TAT
RAT=TAT=TAT=TAT RAT=TAT=TAT=TAT
RAT=TAT=TAT=TAT RAT=TAT=TAT=TAT
RAT=TAT=TAT=TAT RAT=TAT=TAT=TAT
RAT=TAT=TAT=TAT RAT=TAT=TAT=TAT
RAT=TAT=TAT=TAT RAT=TAT=TAT=TAT

misery EMBRACE contradiction PRACTICE
self ENCOMPASSING privilege moral ROT
tirades wobbly SOAPbox more NOT than
SLEEP

                     rigorous shades drawn,
                        carry time streets
                            white noise:::::::::
HISSSSSSSSSSSSSSSSSSSSSSSSSSSSSSSSSSS
HISSSSSSSSSSSSSSSSSSSSSSSSSSSSSSSSSSS
HISSSSSSSSSSSSSSSSSSSSSSSSSSSSSSSSSSS
HISSSSSSSSSSSSSSSSSSSSSSSSSSSSSSSSSSS
HISSSSSSSSSSSSSSSSSSSSSSSSSSSSSSSSSSS
HISSSSSSSSSSSSSSSSSSSSSSSSSSSSSSSSSSS
HISSSSSSSSSSSSSSSSSSSSSSSSSSSSSSSSSSS
HISSSSSSSSSSSSSSSSSSSSSSSSSSSSSSSSSSS
HISSSSSSSSSSSSSSSSSSSSSSSSSSSSSSSSSSS

HISSSSSSSSSSSSSSSSSSSSSSSSSSSSSSSSSSS

.

doorway TraiN platFORM onLookerS
potHOLEs
glances STEal parkS notice winDOWS shuffle
sweatER [good]BYE momentum CHOIR
pulling
FEIGN of ErroR longING DRINKing shark
attacks
exact MISSTEPs take CRISIS conforms
DWELL
(s)(ing)stifles

        finish impulse screen door
        yielded explanation pride
        studying thrown out terms
/////////////////half/////////////////
        absolutes,,,,,,,,,,,,,,,,,,,,,<<<<<
>>>>>skimmed scars & deadened & bleary &
theories
sharpLY flicker madLY sudden
bursts of nowhere lead STEADY
intent overcrowding PASSIVE
proposals CLENCHED earth domes
skin SAGS far(away) accusations=
=peace<apathy>vague+astute+coffeecroissants"
"
[development sTAres stairWELL
shaker(luxuries
time's weary annihilation) solemn PANcakes
walk
sideWalkS shutter shifting moaning THIGHS

10

(whistle?????)]>>>>>>>>>>>

        frozen dripping blanket
        a gate
            tides turning blowing
            a punch . fierce capacities
faint,pulverized,
      barred snails pitiful under
             sentinels   phantom

under
          B E L L Y   creep to sick
     STATUS   quoting " " " " " " " "
seem to MALAISE obsession '' ''
expense reaction class mode TASTY educated
LackING obscured GRAFFITI ruin EXTERIOR
              daily decaying grind(
         onehundredandeighty degrees)>>>>
word HANG moon BiTtEr embracE hotter
differences
differentiate futile [HOTter] paint(ing)(ed)
FRENZY
grrrb grrrb grrrb brrrb brrrb brrrb MUTUAL
power(tower)
                plow <in>[TO]
             crumble money means
             crickets blocks plains
             dogs crashing degrees
             collective case notice
     [N]either[!] howling b/t
        space sponge BLAZing trail,(tail),

cobweb shoes
prove diamond

11

sacred squirming
intertwined lakes
unfurling before
carcass swelling
heat star
index madly

in swelter   over under
hedges brains   blue blue
                    streams subtle glance razor dull
campaign bottom   neck stretched
bottom dulled   summit capacity
                               [conception obsession
                               originate akin GOLDEN
                               flEEced species::::::::::
                                            BAD
                                            BAD
                                            BAD
                               bed,swaying sheets
                    mayhem overbearing typhoons
spilling chaotic INK wine
in battle ABYSS ascertain SPRAIN strain
TrainEd
direction careen untamed
missions,through,outward
strains   of   milky   gossamer
          not a CARTOON ad (in sand)
(stalking) (stalked) (startled)
      hanging   shouting spREE   ignoring
VOICE   softest carnation hoarse
                    tracks&lengths//////////

//////////

12

damp   fields
            stunned
acute KNOCKING ////////// adolescent
CAUSiiiiiiinnnnnngggg

knocking,kissing,avoiding,smelling=burning=ha
ir,,,,,,,,,,,,,,,

                    makes screech door
A(jar)_incessant weather
                         _MarCH+ing tolling
avoiding_fffffffierce
more than BANDAGED hands
SPRING[ing] poison convulsive SNIffINg
    in   relation   to
corner confusion
dream   REALITIES   lounging leather
                  couch
daunting MOUNTAIN
affectation------------
      dayLIGHTS a Hill in sense savings
building iMpaCt hot
GraiN of SanD shredded handprints>>>>>>>
                    folding>>>>>
                    churning>>>>>
                              shades
invitations stubborn
In ComeBack immune SYSTEM refuge
EXPENSE report
labored sparing CRUSH <crunch> <crunch>
mail
under
foot<<<<<
            speeds outlawed

accumulations<<<<<
[prefabricated summations
colored moans baked splintered
wasted   waits remorse BRAMBLEs sweltering
(dis)CARDED hot water jars
]

upside down nobodies PORTRAIT rock
REVEAL groans
MisUse
noun+verb+preposition()()()()()() ""
schematic mazes climactic altogether
incognito folk creature:

average size shaking
swallowing vaguely
photosynthesized haze
LANDfill MUSEUMs comprehension garbage
prosthetic enigma
departure deVOID point rumbling subversive
gases before SPARKLed
pens suffocate IMMERSIVE square root to
CIRCLE circumference SPRAIN
blues ========== incomprehension
========= endless privacy miles
parking
lot agony spirit peril;;;;;;

gulfs b/t computations code language turns blind
fleeting keys shivering beauties / straining
fading imbued simplified trudging / handheld
ding, ding dinging / edgeless facades / caving
two to one ratio / concrete quest microchip
running / curdling clamoring drift off / ring, ring

14

ringing / rumination rediscover language
hoping,,,,,

isolated fang mirage confines fingers
fester diameter splitting snakelike mass
floorboard dimension tone hark!
hark!
hark!
      stones,
         ancient,
    barbaric,reminiscing trajectory sinking
cupboards,,vapor peak,,,
possessive scream,,,, thump thumping
thumps,,,,,gestured squirming
,,,,,,coastal jagged pages,,,,,,,clog debris
blade,,,,,,,,cracks veins,,,,,,,,,
dizzy pointed palace,,,,,,,,,,wall flattened
digging,,,,,,,,,,,

noted METRO era stakes CLAIM amok
PLATITUDES:

                                            self-
destruct in
3
2
1
FUN!!!!!!!!!!!!!!!!!!!!!!!!!!!!!!!!!!!!!!

          changing bridge leaps short
          until. until. until. until. until.
          rolling burst spine completely
          drawers masks equations seals
          bed. bed. bed. bed. bed. bed.
          skulls membranes cryptic verge

15

malady visions rotation spewing
one,
two,
three,
four,
five
FUN!!!

wired   banister heave   ShelteR   hoist
appeal origin story gory imbedded rags
The VERY concept of FABRIC…………..
bone structure megaphone texts
glass necessary throat departure>>>studied
density of a
CUBE>>>
(buildings blew in breeze)
(cartwheels glance chance sidewalks)
[charade middle proof of concept][
satellites crowding
stone age concept/
furious hostage tumble cont'd]
"
folded shrugs COLLECT coded thrust flickering
left ventricle chamber piece spinning on the
turntable carved out of soap venting angry
squirming passages.
"
rub robust dust swagger aggregate
conveyor belt line
stern crutches OLD illusion GLASS simplisTIC
currencies embalm elevators;massages
break protocol;
formula full of BEES;tire iron

LUNG – this jittery tap, tap tapping—
grid HIVE wildest
SENT back SOUP bolted AVAILABLE
bursting misdiagnosed
      propensity standoffish(refuse)[overflow,,,
                utter   ly,,,
                lay in grass,,,
    ponder rendition of an ODE]weird to be
    malfunction=
slipstream sprouted mosaics awkward design lip
look crook
      hate(S) hat(S) stacked inch/corner/nook/
magnifying assist indication limp alley chalk
wall space breeding jargons TOP heavy VEINS
                PoP pOp PoPpinG
ceilings>>>climb>>>STAIRS<<<fl0w<<<track
ing<<<indulge
????????????????????!!!!!!!!!!!!!!!!!!!!!!!!!!!!???
???????????!

FeVeR DeMEAN<or> beAR bare marking
unrequited holeS solution linger FORM
return(ing) penetrate POSSIBLE fossil strife
Wet Essence Vast Well-FORMED Mire TRIal
FiRe LoW HangInG FEnCes shapely Laundered
sheep ReeLinG backOFhead sheetscenes
plANes LoW growl rumble STOMACH [churn]
[spurn] constitute melodic bitter DRIFT futile
KITE infected dystopic match an INSTANT
guzzling harvest BRAIN food NAVIGATION
sprint<ING>,fading solace,daughters guzzle
woes cherished ELBOW market RELENTless
fingerNAIL relic TWILIGHT burns FLAIL
escape starry STARRY flail feet STOMPING

naked never MELTING stinking LENGTH icy
BOOKSTORE waterbed said HAPHAZARD
basic carpet fiber diver striver crashing
teethjawpain stiff chewing underVALUED
flashTIDE hide'ngoSEEK outLOOK station
mastered mist HANGING heavy tied HAT tilt
DROUGHT corner STEAKING trekking
MOUTH astride TOXIC blaZinG three HOLE
punch fastforwarding myth(MEANS)legend
repeat dogMATIC state ASSURANCE eccentric
shapeREshape

Yawns scrunched SORES
pinch ENDINGs nervous
ELEPHANT thingamajig
rigmarole INSOUCIANT
ground control SWING
shift(ING) Tree LIMb an
Arm Scrunches carpool
whirlpool jacuzzi SPLINT
(er)(ed),,,,,,,,,,(invariable)
""knew knowledge noogie
'boogie' "woogie" sloping
foreHEAD dread DOOM
easy chair AVENUE dement
(ed) CEMENT knuckle HEAD
said red salad TONG access
denY spry sigh DRY eye Bye
//////////[rubbing alcohol witch
]Hazel blazing unmentionable
;;;;;;;;;;soon&sooner&swoon
(ing)thin(ner)than (r)(t)ail mark
(ed) SPLOTCHY<drier BONE
shone THRU L'Ymagier WAlK

18

doN'T hOle FloW flooR waking
bakING heir FAD led LATIN the
SymbolizeD initiated WAX bend
MUStache sash,,,,,,,,,ironic ad con
>piety pithy PLENTY historical
nerve ending(s) GASEOUS body
work LIKE sound RHYTHM jut
HuT weakenED problematic job
alliance<><><><><><>BLASTED
OOOOOOOOOOOFFFFFFFFFFF

>innerworkings earthworm critical endive salsa
verde
yes,yes,yes,yes,yes,yes,yes,yes,yes,yes,yes,yes,y
es,yes
sting>>>>>>>>>>>>>>>>>>>>>>>>>>>>>>>>>
>>ing
RaY of riSiNg tide scrolls ENTRANCE
bugaboo zoo

>make merging mentor melt
NO fee vacillates b/t guts
affection[LESS] best [ZEST]
rest WEARY wizened CANE

>VINTage sickness distance POSITIONED
united national SPARK PLUG center
zealous foundation pit GLUG GLUG
CHUG CHUG CHUG % of Thank U

collisions   billboards   amazed
            gusts effect wide studious category
reAligned eager HIGH noon factoid
obsessive charlatans >>>>> philosophical

FREE drink
            & food,last analysis of
        atrocity homework,closure shock
        gathering wire hanger rings soak
        BARNACLES=====:::::

"" "" "" "" "" ""

accumulated boundaries BEMUSE collective
GrOaNs,zones inquire proving GRAY
disMANTLE mantis GloBe noontimes here drop
blade WATER wound PErsIst erasures reinvent
step

  :step prairie sanity
  :pine medicated ball
  :bellies weekend mark
  :qualms excess wars
  :necks shoulder bones
  :soldiers deaf hoops
  :blazing salt refuge
  :affecting penguin thread
  :leeches storm café
  :borrowed expression ring
  :indeed churn pillage
  :factory meditate junk
  :earplug sublime neglect
  :demonic pop speaker
  :material magnetic dreary
  :fans mirror pull
  :glue sick balcony
  :garment conceive core
  :puzzle force gasp
  :radio sniff excuse

:bathtub belch rapid
:blink violence puss
:ping goose nihilism
:portrait sinister bending
:branch tyranny capture
:volcano laugher paralysis
:anecdote pursuit chaotic
:action praxis explore
:page spud cleaver
:testicle spectacle spine
:compose wanting waft
:dig dawn dent
:bark coastal bark
:spark snark stalk
:genetic space sludge
:sled slack slick
:proper classic puke
:outcast bump slump
:pump pit pick
:retire gaze radiate
:learn feather flame
:drink tub bluff
:less show crams
:bagel banter bright
:gem raid pillow
:answer cut pop
:flash fund funnel
:labor twig faulty
:construe construct destruct

option hardly burn consumes standard consumer
spread   false
                      impression,s march observant
   strain,ing   core   escape

swirl,ing   glittery   skin   industry
        artichoke a repair flag tempered
        regulatory tantrum
skinny   awkward
            splendor(inablender)palms psalms
homilies infested conscious age=less melodic
pUnCH
multi   -   modal painstaking farm
  cyclical combustion   talk CARNAGE shop
talk   walk   THRU   raging yarn==

rugged availability,,,specious conundrum
,,,presenting bologna fever tracking,,,ticking

Ye spy
      Ye trick
            tictactoe window
Ye FATHOMless fantastic STATIC bread
POLE
                  worthy beneficiary collapsible
                  pool BILGE bulge BiLe NiLe
child prevents finicky forearm bursting
YE yolk & spoke & ye report authentic clover
DollS
   dollop=wallop,,,serenely basks a DollAr store
curtain RoD beehive engineer sucking
CrabGRASS
            held to yield YE to flee riveting ribbit
squid beyond ye held belief(able) smacking
lip(hip)
,,,drip,drop,ing, sopping wet(ter) bet(ter) neon
out=
patient

yE to squared average perpendicular peculiarity,,,ye
        un=knownnn igloo
promenade,,,pppppplease
to pleasurable prancing ye palace coup YE provide,,,puppy
ppppllllaaayyy(ing) cordless telephoto socket,,,fibula YE
a(VOID) hold huddle MORASS close to POCKET lint YE
    sized MOSS to LaCe Ye to CuRTaiN rod hobby
HORSEshoe>>>YE<<<YET>>>yuck!<<<Not
to KNOt Ye stirrup hiccup(ping) scarlet FEVER
sign o YE time® oven STRAY gutter SNIPE
purr ye purr ye stir potted plant YE copy
COYLY coincidental paper AIRplane gripe Y
e Y e Y E ye prevent suitcase ivory pot to stick snot to
peace(filled)(vast)(last)(ye)YE(y)(E)tho1ce knew need
le in eYE sound of WHICH yak revealed yikes! spikes! spoke
YE did Ye draught yE store/\brand jitterbug slug PLUG(!)(?)
("") ye did malform manifestation measly in least yeast
 break(ing) (b)read <toward> ("") warnING shed
fire(d)   Off BalAncInG act(ion) (re)act
opaque cell YE drain
    dyed PANT leg ye YIP ye FLIP ye SLIP ye BLIP ye
yo   yore   yet
yep

yeyeyeyeyeyeyeyeyeyeyeyeyeyeyeyeyeyeyeyey
eyeyeyeyeye

SPY house ClutteRS shed
land,s plane:::::::::::::::::::

sprout horns & beg merciful nunchucks
soil as they soil
    follow as they frolic
PAN   aim   strike
        fawn   fallopian   feathers
waning   door   crisis   reigns
  slams   lumbering loooooooppppppssssss
frozen white ARROW milk,,,,where,,,,ever
pages palm
d
o
w
n   face CROWDED hint crinkle   of hand
    split PUMPkins spit TAKE manic FORCE
monEy
chugchugchugchugchugchugchugchugchugchug
chugchug
>>>>>>>>>>>>>>>>>>>>>>>>>>>>>>>>>>>>>
>>>>>>>>
appeal MEANwhile ENgiNe;;;close-
up,,,[pre]occupied==
NeaR neAt head
KitChen>'?>>>/>>>WaLl;;;radicalFENCE!!!!
                   abandoned
MELT(ing)(ed)[after]taste(d)
blushes&knock(ed)(ing) RELATABLE less
STEP egoless crutch+++

transparent
GOWN disapproved WHISPER b/T @@@@
%%%%%%%%%%%%%%^%%%%%%%%%%%%%%%
#####,,,:::::
scrrrrrrrrrrrrrrrreeeeeeeeeeeeeeeeeeeeeeeeeeeeecccc
cccccccccchhhhhh
teach CluMP to insinuate custard[loose shoe
variation]endeavor=purse—
mining detergent<"closer
INTEGER*">,,,,,<"caught SHRIMP pure
hand(ed)">##########

destination kiosks AnHouRlAteR attention
s-t-u-d-i-e-s   R   O   W   S   of
chains—
crumble whispers,,hushed,,
useless GADgets,,blank,,red,,
VaGuE gEnErAl misbehave;;
sunglasses disappear / stale / heavy / eerily /
sirens / shutters / tied / flat / dissipate / contact /
town / chug / chug / chugging / remains / have/
full / ecological / pillow / arteries / tundra / blink
/ blink / blinking / tide / washed / smell / jagged
/ potholes / billboards / flea / scam / mock /
cracked / trials / altogether / mirror / recognize /
dizzy / equivalences / float / conflict / sober /
mingling / underground / dialogue / fester /
fester / festering / quash / corrosive / lobby /
cheap / suitcase / tap / gasps / grasps /
suspension / 24/7 / canyon / carnage /
mannequins / pageant / delve / delve / delving /
artifacts / melt / melt / melting / squeeze /
yearned /

blah / institutions / muddled / wander / wander /
wandering / optional / antiquated / soundtrack /
senseless / sink / sunk / subtle / stink / rink
/ grin / hair / outmoded / quick / quick / quickly /
gestured / phone / shaking / sanity / limpid /
facile / desire / rest / rest / resting / grip / of
wander / flounder / throat / uttered / unpacked /
hesitation / untouched / toxic / scrutinized /
neutralized / term / primitive / ear / scapegoating
/ sewer / formless / tight / wire / barb / barb /
barbed / walls / function / deteriorate /
dysfunction / but / material / instability / touch /
touch / touching / fuss / heavily / chance / scale /
speech / less / sinister / sick / reminder / stomach
/ position / waste / disappearance / symbol / ever
/ deep / deep / deeper / backwardness / laughter /
sullen / demanding / small / stone / step /
internalized / tech / myth / frack / frack /
fracking / attributes / muddled / un / concerned /
landscape / besides / cliff / discarded / plunge /
call / presence / line / wing / sing / bring / host /
most / avenged / word / resist / resist / resisting /
backseat / backside / bean / nod / whole / regret
ful / hankering / hunkered / half / disarray /
spray / ground / wail / mid-size / mob / bumpy /
slumpy / pump / pump / pumping / bridges / imp
ly / vigilant / buzz / buzz / buzzing / next / un
settled / screech / beach / sigh / lye / kick / stag
ger / atmospheric / body / stench / inland / styro
foam / method / overlooking / muffin / opposed
sipping / assumption / barking / front / sister /
doubled / clog / clog / clogged / crumbs / couch /
tombstone / busted / rusted / mistrusted / dusted
/ citizen / numbered / numb / bump / building /

unorganized / velcro / paranoia / branch / lock /
attention / retention / tension / envision / attack /
credit / symbols / limbos / nostrils / fabric / atom
izer / blank / slab / unadorned / flutter / shrug /
murmur / nightgown / clown / slick / thousands /
curtains / heavy / intricate / feverish / tool / nod /
rod / sod / fit / fighters / flummoxed / kettle /
settle / settle / settling / tip / toe / wrap / dwell /
aspect / embarrassed / shower / alley / cynical /
trip / backbone / zone / cone / phone / hourglass
/ faceless / cymbal / shotgun / streetlamp / metro
/ compartment / secretion / elation / warm /
warm / warming / admitted / photo / diagram /
intricacy / city / bask / passages / re / jagged /
shack / dusk / overlook / shook / spooked / dome
/ rustle / head / said / fed / red / dead / med / cred
/ spark / spark / sparking / spectacle / paramount
/ preparation / nation / spanking / golden / tacit /
conversation / dim / called / plethora / lid /
bloodshot / lattice / butter / bitter / sit / sit / sit
ting / outline / located / movie / mountain / foun
tain / ersatz / drunk / rose / bumpy / design
ed / disobedience / disregard / happening / sac
rilegious / whimsy / flimsy / what / proud / how
/ crowd / when / grin / why / dry / who / drew /
where / spare / counterbalance / alleviate /
factoid / kite / vitriolic / tuxedo / t-shirt / flick /
flick / flicking / ash / can / spare / parted /
scratched / grasshoppers / pinpoint / stubbed /
lung / drag / exile//

RadicaliZeD bulldozers lip INJUSTICE
like JUICE fLoW terror air SHuNNeD
exposure Empathetic tune ThROaT
ScaRf scarring diametric forcefield

scooter fulcrum humanitarian NeRvEs
knuckled fever blister dimensional
CaUSe=EfFeCt mischief HoUsE
Bonfire ramalama dingdong EaSe
BefOre extremities boost boisterous
blueprints As TooLs shone methodically
elementary InEbriaTiOn dreaded
DraMaTiC invasion legitimate hoLLoW
hello chEEks of legitimate FaCeS amuse
ment Twilights each willing diligence
AsAn extended washing DRIED folded
anagram of LaNd burping CleNcH uN
clenCheD unfiltered heartofthe HEARt
BlaNk SlaTe snake charmed PanTs
lanced behemoth anus human TATTOO
television puppy dog lacerating bLuR
criminal chemical heritage pace in
salivating ANYwhere At PaCe RaCe
broods KicKinG wall hanging airplane
GLUe satisfied hopelessness in WAKE
of AccEnT trouBLED bragging species
unfolding plowshare NOMADIC
outcome squirmed a shift MORE distant
LESS clenched STILL perspective

liked lust crusted spindly bands shatter gross
productive entrail lightly shuffled shimmy
shaking shattered avenging mice coat tails
dressed efficiently eviscerated organically
possessing night spurts deserted highway
groupings commingling guitar thrashed
schoolyard bulletin board graph paper rejects
inky submissive in asp pertained granite
building blocks polymorphous skink beaten

battered banter bending boohoohooing every
way which say gray skinning coat levees weep
cosmic feet creep carp capped million signs
indicate loss gain net proof pudding prisons
poisons darts chocolate box bother defunct
larynx corncob bib branded freckle buttocks
waving proudly airborne shorn penumbra park
bench cinched toaster tasted treated papercut
growling wimple simple pimple dimple buried
new organism orgasm flooded cleansing
web foot deep first frost ape ape lemonade
corners flinch ego scare solid masses goo gone
gripped faucet gyroscope lemon belted bleeding
monarchy rapscallion radically engrossed susan
b anthony coin fountain paint chirps spins bottle
top tube many ludically perverse divisional
bullfighter gorged abandoned less choregraphed
peter pan complex mooned over experientially
unraveled trainline multimillion dollar fine
dandy sandy candy banned until chameleon
returned skeleton radio visitation rites
subversive plumage inferno crystal sighted
prism rule of thumbless engagement velvet delta
alpha missionary spool star forgives dozen
darkened chess piece winding tom-tom persian
gender robe shocks reveals utters peels
simplifies utilizes candlelit ensnared decades
jeweled draconian dent vie before hypnotized
inadmissible period envisions heir shocks in-
person preferred treatment purchased advanced
lined guests state affiliated dementia without
expectations exasperated pigeon carves smack
out of wooden umbrella final funding horrified

classical exquisite erupts moody in long blissed
mystery awash parasitic spy yarn darn exotic
camera crane sang psychology spared self-
inflicted gloom restored parlor organ grandly
realized balding turtleneck crazed foot soldiers
foster care dare hall of mirrors sly nod lost
resume wields onset freezes hysteria commands
spoof unsuitable tasks assigned astronaut
cryogenic speed freak close semi-proof listening
cell membranes mimetic mints blowing up hard
to reach corners of brain matter scattering
expanded inbox thundercloud hotbox grooving
disco pen folding egg-shaped rafters scanned
perching computer id cartoon galactic mission
triumphal illogic anthropomorphic boomerang
clang clang animated innuendo addictive fuel
wiretap union clogging injurious accounting
error glove intervening luxury requires
contractual seepage voicing sleeping outrage
under coveralls successive employment factors
tenfold campaign target panel boot planned pall

Silk scarf SOOTH ammunition prize-winner
old TesTaMeNt on behalf of Boris recon
structed article,,,,favored,,,,allegiance,,,,
NoT,,,,hanging RulerShiP unedited pro
vincial soup scheming hark!!!!! HArK!!!!!
HaRk!!!!! HARK!!!!! yonder sanctuary
disputes embezzlement pyramid chain
facelift ReSuLt surveys LaNd tHeFt gov
ernment initiated Hellenistic archival puke
head edifice ///// cohabitation ///// fortress
///// pinky toe ///// Under[stand]able detail
[s][ed] tOPiC pinhead turbulent revolt

likewise ReJeCT[ion][ed] halo suspect
unethical TeXt substance requirement
verb = NOUN = predict FuTuRe TeNsE = =
fence – two basic eras [ears] – foundational
SLED [epigraphically] a subculture standing
vOICe latter day compatriot FuND chieftain
hedge harbors & SHIPPing DUES & CLUE
S MiShandLEd xxxxx empowered xxxxx
repeat ..... watershed symbiosis power drill
ratified husbandry [house][HOLD][s] clued
ironside rapid adherent frank contradiction
CARE[ful] [full] [time] CORPSE detector
= messianism / formative / prosaic / pester
BERLIN WAlL daDA daDA daDA DaDa
;;;;; ritual CONCUSSIONS ;;;;; FIG lunge
broader CoLoniZeR narrative dim DeGree
>>INTRO [OUTRÉ] [seldom] keep scurvy
,,,,, MeNtIoN weak PaLm ,,,,, cultivation
monographic reflects herb allusions spelled
] ..... [MiSt] [tabernacle] saddle-saddle[s]
Up ..... revelation ErOtiC structure cone
challenge Pulverizes WisDoM care mania
..... lunar AbStrAct eclipses ..... shoulder
(such depiction cultivates allegiance b/t
counterbaLaNcE FooTwEAr & biproduct
HeAdGeAr [fear] [No!!!!!] [knot?????]
SpOt brandish prophetic vexing porphyry
cylinder SeAl[ed] appellate court fungus
WideSpReAD dead [head] [end] [ed] [ing]
vIvId Ezekiel [book] [worn] astonish moss
contrary beat [the] F[o][a]RM yet & yet
SiNcE [beat] the OddS ,,,,,) ///////////////////
focus after renewal sovereign exposure
zapped [ing] language barrier dEAf lEAf

RooF abusive sermon dust spleen turnstile
MiLe [AFTER] mile [before] style ,,,,, [
left evidence decided pencil v[a][e]in
) [. , . , . , . , . ,] tinted cosine urgency race
to BoTToM cArT denounce codified theory
chronological FaLL [famine / strain] ,,,,,
indeed resurrection monitor crap ShooT
cApTiVe minister contains sharpshooter
proclaim a Y[ea]R a period product source
rhetorical hockey puCK checkered kill
corpus demonic proffered eschatology
fragmented sniffs express [m][n]arrow
aspect smOOth baptist lepers WaLk skinny
jeans declared Enoch a eunuch a crooked
ToE pour Deuteronomy illustrated All Flush
time gains WaRt ingests a pity WiG ,,,,,
,,,,, [hermetically] numBeReD bedding
] bred to tenth anniversary standards
titles TeRmeD mutual impact b[iz]uisness
expertise request[ed] filtered international

dubious   foundations   purify
        MaSter   Works
   pious high command stamped
u
n
d
e
r   an assumed microcosm
        , accommodation
                [Vichy]
          [swish] [swish]
   SWASHBUCKLER   in
extraordinary   TiMe   BuCKeTs

sin
    gular , brutal , TruCK
                    load ,
            poured , dispersed
r
e
g
i
m
e fail [FaiL!] > to HouSe
                exploit village
            , [tobacco] present
        [arms]   ,   flushes
jacket
        f
        ew tRaCkeD
                    ReDs [whiteS]
, targeted   LaW brawl
            [crawl] Wall [to]
        WaLL
        verbal   cues
    sub
        sumed
                added
VaLuE   linguistic
    FaRe
            p
            l
            a
            ying
        jester   promise
            occupied
w
a

v
e
s
   landmark pirate musical
feature,ing
         remote   FlEEt
      gate,
        way   priestess
narrow   hErO   lAiD
      arrow
   potteries   ,   feet
s
t
r
a
p   [what does class teach us
      about human capacity for
      cruelty????????????????]
TreMoRs filming   afternoon
                 dwell
t
i
d
e
s   rewrite
       history
             s
             l
             a
             n
             t
             e
             d
grass,

lands,
        s
, assaulted decade
            ultimate
        territorial   Poly
MATH   SloTh

          ,
    prepared to
arrange
            F O U R
        [subservient??]
,   arbitrate lucid
  office
      s
      p
      a
      c
      e
commodity MiRRoRs social
                destructive
        PaTTeRN   , this
                    highest
                CoUrT   considers
pEErS   obsolete
              , dresses
          iN   rAgS
t
r
a
s
h
y   the dominant style
            [culture?!?!]>>
    , NaKeD   ,   sizeable   ,

sculpted
    t
    r
    a
    v
    e
    l writing
authored   deliberate
        contrast
   TreSpaSSinG<< , excessive
s
p
h
e
r
e exclusively demanding
      , published
manifestation
     of FiRsT
        impressions

    ,
d
e
m
a
n
ding   deCaDeS before
   b
   o
   m
   B
   s , worn out
instincts
     engaged

36

forlorn   gate
p
 r
  o
  n   e expedited
keY to the CuPbOaRd
, opinion LiE
        facts AbSoRb
    circumstantial
                evidence
, fear upends complicated
        interrogation
            techniques
, [Fall of the HoUsE of
        perspective
                ],
contrary   imperative
, philosophical sleight-of-hand
        s
        o
        o
        n
    [er] [est]
                printer
            tactic
        senior   entomologist
  scuffs   shoes
        , introduces   mis=
      leading occupations
n
a
m
e   a ShRuB
        a ToRtOiSe,

          broad   THIRST
                    ,
hunger   orbits
                         m
                         o
                         o
                         N
, exploded   PaiD primary
        , choice high
                    [elusive?????]
elegant
        t
        h
        eft   organizational picture

dim [back] log subjects
bean , screens , taints
bodega loose change rim
spigot burial yam-yam
jam[ming] armpits
money traces cigarette
ash[tray] burning in
unconscious finding
navigational month
parade route , burnt
, an envy , energy
ponderous tatter[ed]
drug counselor talk
talk-talk , walk
capitol ideas throat
[new] treatment less
original business action
[pan]cake [par]take
romanticism shower

curtain , rod , target
, too , two , [
foreground bullet ,
reporter euthanizes
] idealistic southern
hemisphere robber
baron lawyers EMS
, talkative , boom
town , bonbon[s]
wake , an , ant
, ground , pepper
sprain[ing] bonafide
east meets west meets
trading post hangman
, deleted , intergalactic
[disciplinary] sidewalk
, track , field goal
aggressive culmination
dog [tired] lost [elude]
stoking coal manager
bungle , thrice ,
lifetime evokes TV
, watch[ful] , drip
[of] sixth one hundreds
fold[ed][ing] dessert
, unavoidable policy ,
wound prideful end
[over]come tear duct
hut , rut , accent
, criminalization of
catnip , greed ,
[main]ly colorful if
invisible , exaggerated
boar indicates method

idea swift[ly] credit
adaptations cure prairie
, provocative upset ,
clothes [less] square rite
graph axis , formal
, pallor , suitable
fjord outside pajama
[party] costume hat
, dresser , disaster
carry[over] estimated
essential hole in one
bacterial proverbial essay
revisit struggle Arab
spray , nasty ,
training cathedral herb
[moderation] power grab
hands , in , clay
collect[ed] travel lungs
letters prevent mailboxes
bunghole earrings rarity
, Halloween , grand
[supplemental] drug use
island hopping propensity
mind edges resilience
, spill , an age
[point] [of] [viewfinder]
vigilant , old , need
, positivistic popping
surprise homecoming
communication suitcase
rocket fuel energy drink
, math , gravity ,
pull[ing][ed] green choke
marijuana bumper sticker

circle handed directly [to]
[from] nocturnal habitat
, rinsed , 2 x 4 ,
wounds patient holster
cancellations undermine
water[park] taped intestine
[boy] [girl] friend musical
nail , hang , slope
, taste , fulfilled
comparative straw combustion
hairy pilfered palm oil
coconut femur crusade
, humanist , poll
handkerchief whippoorwill
countdown , thump
[practice] makes scenery
foreign [policy] imperial
domestic piss trade string
dare , dreary , spat
[upon] cooler [mini] grief
momentum worship huff
puff[ing] hydroelectric skiff
social , chief , stitch
[appear]ing verbose large[ly]
explanation perhaps punch
pride [vanish] appraisal
pumice college soap mark
point , at , which
butter , churn , book
darn[ing] socks [drawer]
receding harvest pill
tarmac shattered juice [
whole number reference
requested] filed pressure

41

,   elevated   ,   twirl
[ing] lunch[ing] honey
[ice]pick evolution   ,
antitrust   ,   sabotage
mono [poly] screen saver
prestigious planet of
viruses   ,   edition
,   cower   ,   pricey
digitized foreskin band
murder journal witness
valley   ,   name   ,   tool
[memoir] levitation saver
tearjerker shuns settlers
,   tight[ly]   ,   danger
bury thighs of steel
blast[ed] airplane seat
,   megacity   ,   limb
[visually   ,   (ex)plained
ism] emulation agriculture
,   piloted quantum ancient
stilt vision of zero version
dull central science grill
[back]wards [out]siders
years present functional
topographical   ,   armor
,   [sun]roof   ,   a
[n]   ,   personification
suppressive beggar edible
church lava dangl[ing]
buzzword boring clarity
blood   ,   in   ,   tyrant
,   recent[ly]   ,   exist
shown curse possessions
ignore balm remember

winner , winter
, weather , teaches
[tone] [fashioned] where
sardine worships aperture
snatch[ed][ing] monstrous
, leave-leave-leave ,
sleeve train[ing] account
surface[s] grandparent ilk
, hour to context ,
dent greeting card lust
[concept] [matrix] edition
, elaborate porchlight ,
collect[ed] verbal rapture[s]

Altered habits and routines

Rationalize gamble rendered IssueS declare
EmiC reSTAte preference Stud if as all-too-
human DO NOT category SusPecT transcenD
arguably standard ISolated dimensions
DemonstrateD reference AbUSEd properly
(again?) account to recuperate dug / dug / dug /
DIG / DIG / DIG / expression LOFTY observed
vine SYNONYM (or at LEAST) reaching AIM
tiMe ItseLF crypto Neither how TO VoLumE /////
follow(ed) OBject reJect aspect "Stumbling"
"outside" CaGe BeaTs boRdeR broAdeER
limitation STAle Fail word critique StePp(ING)
poorly TerMs negate desert prophetic
CONCRETE magical ecstatic MetaPHor dOOr
reinforce POINT such as "to climb" condition
rendition cannot Here-And-Now structural PlaY
examine(D) exceed "SURMOUNT" / "IN" finite
/ beyond CLIMBing how=ever / never=more /
TabOO reported sysTeMs MinI context usage(S)
FiguraTiVe dictionary surpass CLIMB pincH
definition TRANSLATION RoLe structural
DesPitE mountaintop ONLY iconoclastic
COROLLARY rubric ruptures / dissent / forum /
born / torn / blOOdy self- / devoteD / attack
OrdeR / pride irruptive / as / FesTivaLs / implied
rejections / semi - / ritual repetition elegance
CrOsSeS in TuRn substituted what COULD
universal , self- / multi- / CONflate account
"apologetics" USaGe argues Equipoise
B(etwee)N "IMMANENT frame" pairing
ScaTteReD (in)famous emptied / sit / VanGuarD
attached sea LEG foam Shin "routinization of

cuisine" , MuSiC constructive ditch occur Harmonic elsewhere disenchantment DuaL masks suggest=ed lukewarm "legality" (MODE) (of) (available) ligHT precede DOMAIN axis Aging Ages aghast TREATment "intermediate" dimple / TRUST / thrust / suspend / Pardons / is / in / verbal / display (ed) (ing) / emergence "Strain" immanent STANDpoint further , further , abrupt , MaYaN "above the law" BlurreD / burial / Ochre coincides at WhEEl / at HORN / StoRm / FooTprint / against plastic , pictorial , level FASHION binary "...new paradigm..." limited laser LaDDer latter shot coeval SpheRe temporal LAG Into Much complexion SUBLIME hard-to-fake "selective pressure..." minus height COOKinG price ProCurE natioNaL unappealing origin pursuits FAKE vigorous currency , arpeggios , of , rippling smells SurrounD bulbs ChewinG bean Two Centuries Animal Insider terMs "shitting" camphor fantasy Admixture center PiLe of BreaD counteract realM scholarship URINAL /.../.../.../ activities BaSe reservation CentraL material abstain , mean , Elect , Body virtuosos , Parody INversion Exhale(D) clutches elect force-fed stressed Kitsch to KINSHIP to laity a survival map GUISES sufficient "FIT" big TeeTh or ClaWs / double-mannerism , twice contingencies , obeyed , bindING PoLity scale KING autonomy MeaT aforementioned precious Rise OF .

blubber bath[e][ing]

mused yet another alas P.S. could aware a science
letter [drop the invitation, translator helmet,
dandruff baseball threatens, a disappointment]
truth inferno aardvark favorite law [book,
disadvantage, curfew] litter an impersonal font
less sooooo remember print[ed] become a study
[vet, boring, PSSST, mailbag, sync a yellow
factory] look out chicken the door is getting
sleepy actually attacks an also badge recent a
captor [caverns pixel veggies, blobby, stray,
organism proof, because drives suspicion] age of
ruthless contents zipper [zapped] hypnosis half a
running start [platypus, patron of lost groaning]
gravity has a blue period a hug jumbo orbiting
expression [cubism called & wants to extreme,
sulfuric acid clouds, presumably melted, assured
launch] wrapping roving canvas sparks cicadas
aboveground baby crawl at once screeching
spotted false [brood X conceives handwriting
head] unlike bodyguard tree roots appearance
patterns learned paralyzed santabarbaraite uses
flexible tongue [contains iron, meatloaf, gun,
called a boot, fever pen, 90 lungs per cycle] brawl
through grassy glands tiny layers of shell
provoking engrossed extracts fade alluring
bounce across a mint leaf beetle [shine ridge,
absorb electric sums, flavonoids to figments]
production wings energetic century butterfly
mixing shellfish [will turn] milkworts are pink
[vivid band of textiles] accidental process scoops
a teenager unlikely raw mauve refashioned as
chemistry [donned engineering bites, failed] self

a pigment drenching afforded compound
synthesis made done substance sampled [lava,
quotation, scaled rub off] walnut perfect gullible
hesitation obvious language sinew [glorified
"stinky" , abstract "skunk-like" , personal
"gasoline term"] regardless eyesight dulls
evolutionary pride decimal an impactful breach
without traction shaded key to credit card
[hailstorm] numbers virtual popping mystery
[color-sensing] computerized comb tears the
scalp strongest optic complimenting pair [wheel]
artistic anchor [like saturn] repeated rules
fascinate preppy [w]hole [lately] renowned trick
box cutter rainbow manifesting urgency
withering coronas blocked an example [i.e.
irisation,, iridescence] clear electron flashes
venus message from mist [or] [and] [if] [when]
[then] [...] [...] enter droplets reverses lighted
rare moon [massage] [...] parahelia horizontal
event

boogie-woogie

melanin sources mottled forest floor giving skin texture running gag membrane microscope , fossilized shape observes bacterial curation whenever bleak bipedal scales revert , tiny turns of feathered tastes sanitize drab , leaping said ::::: "study might night dwell signaled surrounding helping extinction" ::::: non-avian habit of coating mask , busybody relevant shimmering climbing spiral skirt staircase grin , next nest may ascertain creatures , length soils habitat , wiggling must offer an explanation ::::: "universe detects combined filtered hues as if transported by famous infrared renditions short for human colliding" ::::: tongue Jupiter representative otherwise , pinpoint a nebula , upper equator like a pulse , visible gathering pancake , will be flat , will be layers overlapping , tubular , chemicals painting bathroom in time without extreme , most populous semiprecious , corrosive , less sickening , waning name not a good mineral , spectrum knows that words vile ::::: "cave walls discover less a carefully manipulated psychology advertised before conveying brooding authority" ::::: white sees a funeral , issues solid statement of absolute , youth warms to chaos , filters separate labels from necks , would-be testing and insects absorb "flowers of death"

freckled fumigating all-around lint

vulnerable contest makes a sound. practice walks without heavy lifting. toss a lid to chicken crossing shrug. being elegant suggests a trick. stubbed toe cockatoo brains a common measure. facing suggestion. figure a wombat. something warm compares skulls. drifts. modernizes. tinier humans carry sensors. video camera odor. vibrating band of assholes tempestuous. grinding 1,000 times a second. reliable lips cup practice fires. hollow plucked pubic hair marches. plectrum. spectrum. twang. plink. sharp squeezing bellows air conditioning unit. maximizing ceremonial rattle. meet rich. cut wood. drastic violin choice simplifies dish. dried sap. power of a brushed flexible membrane. wavy. flash.

warm[ed][ing] over coal compress

one wanders Greek in prospect puzzled over
scratches balmy touching flinty reserves jammed
finger length between arbitrary escapades
archaeological in jacket bottom variations fenced
steel dimension fishy like wheels perversely
plagued clever enough to wield an exception
accommodating phantom bifocal timber pulling
leverage acidic core lapping rubber band an
encapsulation punk pricking montage realized
forsaken formatted tag you are out to boundless
sacrilegious dancing a KaBooM! a HURRAH!
that quits before lunch minces wordless after
breath stable country allusive island ashes what
trading supplements through rudimentary open
hoses banging ashes less an assortment special an
address book royal as a gulf ensures blasting
planetary chatting to pry to set to loosen to chatter
one ear clapping while another threatens stability
in the meat trade whining fur lined cavity finished
favored released after pause sumptuous to
tenderized glaring league.

bOmB dAwN

FlOOd the SquIdS & vAsT NeSt cOvErS spinach
As It LieS gEsTuRe free but LiMp / gOOd FalL
AlBuM w/ BeeS a BeNcH hEAriNg / sEEk
NoT So ThaT You'LL be SoUgHt AfTeR /
released FrOm RoCk / sTEePeD iN CareLeSS
indiscretion / SPeNdiNg / SlaPPiNg /
HaPPy as a DaY gLoWinG / gleaming off
SuSpeNdeR bridge / controller / hOOked by
CrooKeD / listening to VINyL shinbones
avalanche a taste / GLUEd promised LaNd /
LaugH / AS YOU laugh IT / MaY ALL
engineered EnIgMaS occur in simultaneous
PopPiNg / PlasTeReD / cough /
COUGHING / By MaKe Or MeAsuRe /
totem piled to DeAth

castigation natural selection biproduct easing

confidential apartment dome struggle for success frozen in between self-congratulations and glowing proverbial dampness running down the lines. too fine to be a fiber. secrets are less than ball and chain communiques tho busted flattered than a symphonic cinematic decision. left unmade. sympathetic to degree of difficulty. passing Beirut harmonic oppositions rocky to beached argonauts. leading friendly. little squirrels of crystal say the public is an algorithm. their fathers soil their wrenches. if hearing an entrail stored up from loving. gone and never existed. former. fathomless. an accordion regurgitates noodles. may anyone else attach an anniversary.

sectioned carapace makes a xmas card sing

light controls a fixture / a craze ,,, do not disturb
/,/ pine smells chest at least left laughing //
reinvented sweetheart treats tombs to oblique
preference ,,, all the treatments kingdoms
squander in their vast squalor /.../ listen to phone
machine rock opera spreading cherry lips
notational device rampant from See to shining
SceNe stolen balm ,,,...,,, mousepad philosopher
pardon but teeth are serendipitous in the rain –
SHOUT ELECTRICAL SOCKET PROVERB
[less ecclesiastical] [so-called vain treatment]
PLACED DUMMY ON A CURTAIN –
imploded plaster caste formation ::: By OnE bY
TwO By bye ::: [product of fiddlestick ginger ,,,
snapping nail across great war of famine soaking
pea] ... present corresponds over centuries with
seedless flowing intestines / buried foliage
understands as much as touching can obscure
/,/.../,/,/ lightning alley unguided ,,, INTO
EMPIRE they crawl [...] briefly modern /
painfully obvious / embrace a WoRlD myth as far
as you can spit ,,, siNK tobacco in to the imperial
butt cheek / grind / gnash / solitary castle works
wonders ,,, battles ... abridged so as to skid less
vapid than faraway /

spiral evaporation device

divided commentaries sudden event-based only mundane underrated INSTEAD distinguish disintegration undercutting vocabulary (fear of mirrors) blurring said circumstantial imperviousness (sadism? heritage? gothic? as oblivion?) memory accepts subjects qualities silliness as overlooked as entirely an allegory (tabulate edicts) enabled chromosome by land by urban by ennui by articulating parental tires (range of candidates anomalous specks) daughter essay guesses residual documentary seething compression mocking as a hunter transforms manuscript into cannibalism (sprouted basement hunger, recovered photo augmentation) still less productive than gum tho reimagining fungi (evidence as ambiguity) change remembering to replicate rupture (rhyme? preoccupation? foreground? insistent?) no less claim than linear NOT progressing NOT consuming NOT extrapolating (fact an agency of bitterness) in reserve meaning define disorder play ecophobia excessive rank brevity (presuppositions) TOWARD (genre) WITHOUT (memento mori) DISGUISE (fault) CRAZY LOOPS (riot) ADDRESS (subjective simmer) DEMARCATED (bedecked) fantastic attraction an impending anxiety (sensation? assertion) dissolution

made of refunded sheets

how itself found mountains... hard sin a turning
point... did have borders backwater... lawless...
crosswords... engaged dress declaration...
richest uncertainty... tomb relative history prays
legacy... or earth... in spatial dust... return 99
have crossed 88... recent recorded classical paths
host erection... documented cemetery... unless
soon diaspora collects... remembrance taboo...
abnormal detachment... foreseeable line naval
warfare solidified aspects... coalition singed
conquest kilometers... sang cut sophisticated
grip... insular campaign defeats undermanned...
fleet defaulted decline... symptoms survey
impressive periodic conclusion... zealous
implement laboratory... carte blanche evening
legal basis... crackdown antioxidants... of
tribes... of place... prompt halt bombarded... to
have 54 murders appointed governor... first
attributed refusal... shrewd bouquet contain
archive... unchaperoned field gaps &
mysterious... even reciprocate questions
disagreeable... call it skeptical bequeathed...
descendant scorns deduct... illiterate lowlands
enamor climbing... careful bears... frozen waste
solace tormented... exaggeration reveals court
versions... habits of inquisitive tower... inclining
barnacle... a look... verify a hue... tycoon
handshake blockade... industrial hunters
shame... rule... three-legged libation...
subcontinent outsider characteristic nutshell...

portraits,,,,,conflagration,,,,,retraced,,,,,delega ted

over dollar,,,,, neither wave nor splinter supplicated hand,,,,, are you a streaming lotion swimming without hide or hair????? & seeking stormy beatitude lashing against seldom sparkled rain,,,,, a point shouts,,,,, any ever remoter than a hail or balk of stone embracing eked out living nauseated client,,,,, tell a tale a telling treat,,,,, to sisters!!!! to brothers!!!!! no aunt can uncle a nearby sightline crawling from its gesture flat,,,,, much navigates yet dealt a shawl,,,,, ample shaping nightshirt squawks,,,,, early christened experiments due course evaporate,,,,, to change,,,,,[…],,,,, culture phrases attempted reshuffled master bankrupt,,,,, others added,,,,, no more true [tho] information regards [itself] in stubborn mirror extension,,,,, them[selves] acute to deal in signs nautical,,,,, outmoded annotations instrumental fraction expound judgments [with] [in] regard [to] available validity [main],,,,,[…],,,,, adverse pretext coaches situation blush,,,,, leave something upper as immediate used whole seem[ing] implantation,,,,,[…],,,,, closed myth the mouth imbues willy-nilly tangent,,,,, [run],,,,, patience occupies lack that demands illustrative [f][r][a][g][m][e][n][t][s],,,,, toward further octopus direction includes scale buffered destinations,,,,, wherewithal essential employed syntax,,,,, [less a syllable meandering],,,,, once referred to wandering,,,,, twice convinced pattern,,,,, […],,,,, further obeying marks pastiche deliberation,,,,, endless posturing nature in exchanging horizon,,,,, [belonged] [score] [each] [pause-mask] [dearth] [quote] [change],,,,, prevented steamship magazine,,,,, indebted seafaring persons sort of sounds,,,,, relevant efficiency,,,,,[...],,,,, into thusly provokes limited atmospheric attempt,,,,, asymptomatic perseverance coating throat licorice trapezoid,,,,, vainly glorified sandwich of a future tracked,,,,, [miniscule] [raided] [having] [half] [a] [judged] [walled] [declamation],,,,,[...],,,,, clipped runs the square to sail bottom wafting upheaval,,,,, once a port of grammar stacked in reference [#] eleven,,,,, yields a bullet toss,,,,, portent withdrawing tentacles quick as incubus phase of pool,,,,, squeeze [a] phrase central,,,,, tantamount to treasonous frustrated prophetic hall,,,,,[...],,,,, & outside the city,,,,, parenthesis,,,,, hold the portfolio the key built contrasted to immemorial

MiSSed Connections SuPplanT

ProduCt of spill reNt VaSt circl(ing) SunNsPoTs
sodden household objectified kinetic MoNsTeR
hones in on VeNuS trappED b/t RoCkInG
HORSE & if since DriFt as A puzzle Opaque
LiMits AdvancING dye JoB tOld quit LaCk
BacK OvaL OWL matrimony marionette washed
AciD duSt on AlbiNo surfboard in HoarD
hisTorY stuTTeR sTePs PeSts (blow that windup
TOY bIrD call lament a RanCiD coAt ArMeD
full w/ glacier. w/ coma. w/o instep. Fred Astaire
HaIR   (piece?????))   this   WiSH
a…a…a…an…an…an…fructify   BeNcH
warmed BeYONd aLarM perks CoFFiN enigma
SiGnaL intercontinental LiBerTy Freudian SleeP
MaSk curtain RoD tOnaL garden EatiN' for
Beneficial sultry sexual cardboard MaNiFesTo
DeNteD doughnut hOle sewn INto Vermouth
VerMoNt MaINe shaTTereD recorded stream
blasted proverb reinforces sinkhole phantom of
the GrIMaCe kiSS Kiss bye-bye birdie hurdy-
gurdy ToileT FluSh swish commissioned for
commissary OrDer a BeeF leaf SPlit the BiLl
wInDoW willS foregone conclusive PieCe
poetIcLy breakneck Spasmatic PuRplE heart
once gestural picaroon GiAnT teasing TenT pole
Ant Sandwich drenched oil BoIl toIl soIl mole
memorable synchronicity bone flutter fettered
father SON Holy BOAST toast of ToWn at
sledge Dredge Hammer SauCe BuRRoWeD
CroSS zoological creeper Jeep beep-beep-beep-
beep WaKING pinball TreNcH averaged OuT to
MeeT great WALL of lament doesn'T cost a

58

CeNt transplanted giant Instructed HeaTeR fired
Napalm son of the daughter of the grizzly open
ENDED wound PaTroL NOT french NOT
religious NOT liar liar pants split at the Back
suicide MaPle TrEE Baltimore Ave. Trolley track
DON'T look buck (eye ground GRADE A
muscle builder shield) LASERED UrbAN verge
of Rural FeeDing reproductive gallon WaLLOOn
a SpooN too too too SooN maladjusted MeMorY
bank in THE tank less StooD then a MooD
invoking hooligan breathalyzer BiBle BeLt
restricts FloW JoY heaving plastic meteorite
carried pincher PRINCESS priceless pardon
DeCaY divideD premise preening perpendicular
BeaRd of BeeS.

long-time dissolving puncture

sleeping sleeve. exacerbating. room to which
does not belong. bicycle cavalcade pipe not
operation. switch. control proverbial glow. ing.
shatter. ed. vamped shivering milquetoast.
skimmed. skimmed. tho change purse. pursued
cowboy manhole. cover. ed. ing. beams beaming
basking lilies. sort. ed. proof. contagious garden.
fair. ly. magnolia pleasured. wing. choir stoop
detail. cave. hear voice raisin. raised. razor. oasis
diaphanous sheen. mock. ed. ing. chrome outline.
chalk. carpet talk. circle. circle. circle. cycle
renovated sharp. attack. ed. ing. tact. ful. out
think. occur. spare pushover brawl fair. ground.
ed. universal potpourri. cent vicious. hit. nail.
bed. in. stead. pinnacle waved through. carpenter
length. at. liquid fever pitch. ed. ing. cliché
backwards out solves crisis. jump. s. ing. suit.
head. board. hunter. with. out. in. yelled color
wheel. spoke cow linguistic hound. ed. baby
crawl first space moonwalk. surface schism.
sinew. to-new. two. acoustic food cellar. slat. ed.
risqué lazy parkway. lemming pretends cabinet
telephone. least pound. s. ing. preparation
apocryphal. circulated glands. refraction sweat
gland. heel. s. apocrine. molecular follicle arm.
pit. cubist pubic region. cytoplasm denoting
association. droplets. fat. flag. pole. steely pearl.
classified term subtype. anatomical. nervous
numerical plug. an. overview. an odor. an. an. an.
an. once acted perspiration. directly core
abundant. scalp chronic direct. ed. ly. fund found
requested optional. capture territory. repeat

topical niche. epidermis. coil lowers duct. indistinguishable spices. budding inactive embryologically impersonal. stood. state. d. statue. arousal keratin tissue. trigger. ed. ing. imbalance fetal war. casual. not. apart. sort. ed. horizon. specify apathy. presence involvement site result ranging. 1. to. 200. to. specialized not. inflammation. occlusion. acne retract. s. ed. ing. sinus cacophony. rare. are. malignant. teach chapter remote access. pro. study. globe. libel affair. this. blood. litter. an. oath. overt reformation. station. defeat. ed. ing. life implicates rush. ing. generational letter. lack. ing. ed. space. identifying. worldwide. viola. can. not. storybook. how arriving buy make today. $.$.$. defy chameleon with. beath did trade insult. ed. becoming decision judge. wires struggle. paunch. embittered gone civilized itself. ?. %. #. $. !. over. dose. island edition experiment. first declassify. not recovery untreated pleasure. mess.

dust releasing outdoor cage

youth illuminati a return   pants entrench
storybook regalia   anthem pressing against
breast plate   an absurdly robin bug   intimate
rain fools perishable rug pulled out from banner
locking jaw begs pardonable untranslatable
brassy redemption   piece of peace pleases
pleasurable bull back to board chalking plunge
the collected egos of a million kings   whip lasso
suited up to meat ground khaki   paying off
paradise of bred endorphin control group
     resident lace   silky flummoxed assassination
return to nano vessel effector

compared attack of salient plagiarisms

stiff coddled watch hands evaporate dogs / least
would be zipping with Phantom of the Opera
death toasting population decreased finale
resembles B sharp flat note of blissful awakened
angularity / bike riding meant words uttered as
whiplash / guarantee / before antiquity shrugged
/ an envelope of fleshing pro semantic wrapping
paper bellowed / : / "innocence weeps because
there is nothing else to do and sand regenerates
poison concentration strain" / already laundry
room exploded with proverbial instigated
castigations / while a horn stammered / : / "be not
less wise than rent can be paid nor suggestable
least obscured holiday trashing post" / tho
stomachs always pay for it one way or another /
thwacking mainstream pyromaniac kneels before
the great admiration of industrial revolution
despair and whispers / : / "but why go on without
so much as a technicality to back up all that's said
and done as head splitting air overwhelms
undertakers and charlatans" / oh the well from
which springing brands iron lung / squared
obedience symptomatic migration / period of
rapid decline / beauty eyes the uninvited
acknowledgments and says / : / "sobbing ceased
all its worthless ballyhoo" / to wed / to witch / to
wield / scanning outbreak flute solo / trap the
notebook / the socket / the leaping that preserves
stranglehold / crumbs galore / and more

bombarded a terse battery

instant RAFT brain PLEASURE circuit COPY
>>> tracing BASKETS enlarged PLATFORM
[merchant dialogue] , [contemplate ratio] >>>
watercolor RENDERED erratic DISPOSAL
stones ARRAYED eroded >>> [as defeat
viewed] , [reclaimed jurors] , [indemnity tactic] ,
[warfare thereby] >>> general JUNIOR civilized
LOOTING break ROCKET launched
HATCHET >>> [invaded spot] , [town
elaboration] , [blurred fire map] , [hat consumed
crown] >>> citizens OCCUPY bulwarks URGE
operational FIXED coordinated PAVILION >>>
[affirmed surfaces] , [structured motion
committee] , [main hanging recess] >>> gilded
SKILLS weather DEBRIS sought OMITTED
improvisation CANVAS >>> [sheets disappear
flame] , [speculate compact companion] , [odds
suspect reunion] , [fixtures flagrant mangled
peripheral] >>> sparing FIXTURES enter
EXAMPLE said MOST allegiance SIGNALS
paraded TREK paying KNIFE permitted CAPER
managerial SHREWD purloined KNAPSACK
oddly ESCAPED rolling TUBE revoked

alchemical slapstick card counter

dead letter toast town drunk survival kit
<common detonator purses thin walnut lips at
least standing tree trunk drunken hymnal flooded
whole ailment gesticulating promiscuity> tested
lustful transmissions telegraph bookends granite
spoken like a true nincompoop dressing for din-
din party store swimming <kite flies typewritten
manifesto akin zeitgeist visceral pun scab on a rag
in the sad town synchronicity club car sandwich
gristle> not hanging tho harrowing huge
installment of paid castle parachute as a pinwheel
gross until monster pools children ,lite wand hair
cesspool barcode long as autobahn sharp as
endearing scrolling locked door pertaining fenced
same-same blaming solstice/ almanac must occur
tho breakdown

circle of atmospheric piano

single stroke embedded armchair of no consequence willing the exhilaration of supposed telegram criminals bloodthirsty when introduced to single striking of deported peninsula pity. several contained subjects suppose themselves as spiraled situations plunged without deserted production trials recommended vast number of howls. dispatched central village units purge nomads as a project taken hostage as discontent violates catastrophic function of logistics. anarchy overcoming purchasing power. burden fells expensive drought instead of incubation. incorrect stenographic disputes arm weakened instruments uneducated in particular network erasing clutches. henchmen simplify universities. course of collective disloyalty integrated into degraded terminology. neither precious nor controlled. manhunt resides in the compelling taxonomies of instigated conspiracies. disposed teeth knock shadows off decimated contradictions. encrusted axiom builds road to junkyard broken throughout reunification waterparks. panicmongers flee mural with a leaning style included in an escorted discourse. pigsty shouts waterproof report. loaves steal organs. blockade uses shield to humanize temporary sanatoriums. hotel landscape for purchase. palpable grew and grew and internal a yardstick vantage point without resurrected empire.

woven into matter

Perennial newsPrinT radicalized sMeaR schmeer NearLy trapP,iNG trip flipping contextual subtracted spooky Remnants Suffocating JOURNALISTIC cup o cup o cup 00000 then poWereD Step UP exercise Gulf StrEaM jockSTRAP evolutionary imperative PinCH toWARD elementary detective BoTtLe OpeNeR card GaMe count (ed) (ing) counterattacked DaWN's neatly puking (water)(wishing)WELL spray having SPRUNG a hanky spanking gentlemanly RUSE in the LaPeL swine FLU w/o SoUp remedy wink(ed)(ing) persistent QUICKsand pleasure in DesTrucTioN news anchor head COLD loser Bruising BaLd lackluster Justice of the PEACE seeSAW haul crawl maul doll coarse BiBliCaL shudder jitterbug re: , re: , re: , re: , re: , re: , re: , re: , re: , re: , The MuMmY regards itself in MiRroR imaGe chalice with YaRds to Go Before confrontation SeaL of Approval moves pubic sentiment beyond MaSS graVeS and bobbing for COAL dust POKING through sWaB swap ancestors SqueeZe inTro VeLcRo bike shorts SpLittInG atomic serenading Zorro horror sparrow staring through TypeWriteR ribbon at TimeBomB finite chorus breath mint seeking Refuge from harpoon.

antecedent habitable sparing stage of preposterous duration

texture doctrine intermarrying tissue called obliterated system & sunday archiving erudition tactile as a leech perhaps heavily utmost wave alliance silver beam a whole cult of threads;;;;; uttered dynasties mystique single found city-state gust of specimens;;;;; generations risk ceilings to manufacture ill-suited rejoicing particularities <"half million elections better propositions caged encircled application,,, main causes merry-go-round,,, degradation severs pardonable price of events">;;;;; double illusion or shoulders equally collusion pauses mastering word jokes grand enough to defeat capitalists;;;; sabotage situated refined argumentative publicists;;;;; wanted infecting order blares disorganized organism <"ring a carnal digestion espoused by because owing to temporal treatment of ritually isolated stomachs">;;;;; lassitude echoing stone and law pre-figured dead season dirt losing leak;;;;; position involuntarily suggests nourish and harbors inextinguishable supple magistrate;;;;; lacking infinite culpabilities contrary to an unburdened typography;;;;; exaggerate judges offer heresies to the more distinguished hours <"the least falsification redeems exterior disaster an intercoastal time,,, profitable laziness confounds groundlings,,, shoulder forced born lapse literally consoles long avenues then die in interval">

posterior location space

:: vacancy of throat :: utility of time :: existence
spooling collectable happenstance pile driver ::
tureen cantankerous class system :: arbitration
sponge :: mistreated automatic whiplash ::
advantage melon baller :: purse shoots vomit
talent show :: storm paddywhack hole in solemn
bark :: foliage percentage commentary :: zone
troop neck welt :: bad form :: gamine prevents
third world dictionary fair :: grammar military
coup :: cuckoo :: packed purple dysfunctional
magazine :: back brace addendum :: projectile
immobility :: impose accustomed social
guillotine :: incapacity sketch :: parrot
rationalizes unity :: presupposed tulips :: caravans
qualify world-weary sublimity :: responsive body
hair rasps :: mocked sex mutation :: generalized
hard-boiled deduction :: peeled wished hence
invested transformation :: unfettered seeing-eye
dog :: vice-versa vantage magic :: preposition
accomplish prestige :: association skimming
category of non-factoid bruised fruit railroad
mirrors :: gesture swarm structure :: speak
employed eucharist fair :: monopolize opacity ::
subjugating discarded routine flow points ::
protested discarded recursive element :: bleated
jam foot :: moaning wing :: cheese spike earnest
geometric nudes :: craters poking reindeers ::
aspirational vertigo :: linked soaking visionary
siesta :: cipher of ethical reconnaissance ::
germinating navel :: filth butchers spectator's
slop bucket sport :: drain the blood of fries ::
spittle top hat :: sundry salamander hiccup ::

disoriented synagogue :: terms direct cooling agents of choice hallucinated vegetables :: hall soup century :: productive panoramic confrontation :: priest reproduced as dorsal cavity :: subdivided to house the brain :: tunnel of anatomic legibility :: fluid mainlines a housing project :: cement envelopes spinal location :: tendency to radioactivity

petrifying vibrations in miniature lab coats

>a hook left in the cage

the shaggy soprano stubbed sushi pole reinventing rhinoplasty in flossing leaderless antebellum as superior as a numbed honk aping check book pier of imported Gertrude Stein wine

>>lopsided staircase leading into the horizon

sultan of seesaws checks into a conch shell only to discover phantoms living through bronze age butt cheek carnivals covering lampshades with skin tags with enough cabbage left over for coconut brain swelling

>>>sudden burp of manhole cover

filtered rags make a magic piled higher than an airplane graveyard philosophical in point of factual police brutality between earth shattering lantern skins folded into eighths and run under faucet cotton swabs as a broken arm carries the two and soles for ecclesiastical rage

>>>>lumberyard process of enlightenment

cinnamon oh cinnamon cannot be less than an underground atmosphere mostly wearable in an out of doors beehive clover splayed against three piece sound collage cricket

>>>>>>naked nights on mars

smokey the bear trading cards a zebra stripe painted on a loading zone canary yellow refrigerator door just to make a handstand a special occasion anniversary gifts wooden opaque drenched in recommendation heart throat operas

>>>>>>>*uppercase woodlands revisit jazz standards*

attacking milestone soil sent a foolhardy squire trembling down a sloping sesame seed exact in measure of liquification while also teethless without check and balance degree changing megalopolis primary care physician

>>>>>>>>*pardoning flower in lapel humor*

by means it was and were it to shrink spuds and all then where and why as much as meets the eye a pie a dung making miniscule symphonies flog themselves regardless of provenance and without the variety of knuckle sandwiches that oyster fed preachers had once hailed as the greatest of all football game massacres by the time the alarm sputters there won't be a dry horse in the hut

dislocated calamities train in swirling palms

]part paucity engrossed CreDiT PoLiCy StuMbLeD pi to degree umbilical cyclical nano evaluation technique formLESS apparatus [attach,ments = loose ends = fragrant phrases = meander = astonish = exhaustive = posthumous = dissident] >>>>> points particular peculiar pointed WiDe-RaNgiNg ShAmE CuLtUrAl products mobility of DeSiRe SpUrTs OuTwArDly // willing(ness) notches impassive disinfectant // TunInGs aTTacHeD to rattling // contrary fossilized estrangements >>>>> [odd,ity = relentless = enraptured = enormous = ragged = pressurized = twisters] >>>>> ONstAgE disabuse LooKiNg GlAsS // skull spouse optical formulation hours flattering contrarian // reverse identities sufficient vintage // out AppEaRs cLEAr aN ErRoR uNcAnNy >>>>> [dance = detective = wear,able = adjoining = proclivities = skip = conditioned = supposed = generic = prior = trousers here a only serf cured] >>>>> frisking BaRd rural ExTrAcT myriad degree INIMICAL contrived lyrical subsistence // semester alcoholic to weave a wave to acute exhibited podium // thrilled correlation socioeconomic blackBOX sock domination demonization exploitation >>>>> [solitary = end,less,ness = banana republic = attend = digressive = valence = shrieking = pressurized = likewise = sanitized] >>>>> PreSuMeD overHeAd motorcycle SwInGs ambivalent PSYCHODRAMA first time lewdness gives COMBATIVE measured for splitENDs an EcHo

methodically subjective

culprit concludes anomaly drawn through decreasing reversal of source robust cheek reveals hypothesis charting iterations creating blank imports in questionable salvage enforcement risks naïve data unique narrow dispersion a monthly standard deviation feature median % of excess misleading outcomes distribute software malfunction covariances without exorcising demonic drawbacks disputed version simulate randomness assumptions sense duplicity conundrum unanticipated anecdotal lingering attempted statistical personality disorder

suspended rearticulated confluence

dismantled [working] line / colors // rhythms ///
prosodic shrink [field of approaching ideological
genres] >> impulsive comparative possibilities
[BIG mutation holding GlObAl mourning] // all
aspects an impulse to compass,, early MODERN
to contemporary COMPLAINING::::: "regard an
elegy as transatlantic accumulated through an arc
tho NOT a book instead hear a PRIVATE mist
settle a SCORE" [lines revisit casual
counterpoints less degree than fruit] >>
BEWARE the FASCISTS everywhere!!!!! >>
literal strumming link [brink of source] / earthy //
casual /// flirtations with assassination squad
[chainED educatED burden] >> in theatrical,,
regional jail cell,, SeCoNd ANTHOLOGY /
murky [masks] complete nomenclature
[signifiers] without correspondence // steal
definitive disconnection /// laborious tract >>
[lighting a simple dog],, who tells clusters
looking inward::::: "cease entire flabbergasted
canon as developed by outlived FORCE
positioned unaided in WAR inside an extracted
DEPTH regarding irresponsibility" [score a
quarter return to shame help a critique] >> this
side of constellation creates torn-page
phenomenological concern / melt discipline //
recall stand plants /// celebrate disinterest >> style
[reproducing] bilevel predecessors [point of
view] expedited dispute [poaching accuracy]
welcome resistant abandoned lyrical CONTEXT
[homage] flush [tie] occasional accord clarified
touching

containing languish less frivolous

coined vibration anticlassical fashions an insult
paronomasia based like ship on rhyme then
ammunition nobility proper to alliterative
departure // humor busting mocking beasts
privileged washed snowed in subjective
confusion the fruit of conflation state of
arbitrariness underlines violent pun // a hat // thus
ironic dancing queue disjointed question discerns
audience gloom wit of sensibility dependable
chanson continual shifting attack placement root
// concerned associative words as plausible values
// cadaver imagines interested patterns // owing
toothache box shield comparable diluted to whom
it may dissuade // basis medieval ontological
punctuation exploitation machine // accented
breaks terrorize misquotation // recycled spree
deeding synonymous punchlines // vignette
confessing incestuous idiom a lieutenant
described before irrevocable recurrent firing
squad ball of wax // protocol reproaches all that
heightens expressive conflicts // effect paradox
faints in frenzied pronoun head cheese // out of
vagaries contracted characteristic landfill //
inscribed inappropriate entrapment unstoppable
drain telephone hearing scenario fratricide brutal
as conflicting bashing doll throne // therefore
terms moderate defamiliarize drunken donkey
without a neighbor suggestive of crumpled up
assemblages //

spheres switching epiphanies

thresholds hidden perpetual uncover deciphered
pre-texts demand slated blindness ventured
doomed allegorical progenitor figure telling
crucial extended corollaries another viewed true
tenuous name plastered invented unfolding
universe fail a mission bask partial befuddle
idealistic mediation as elusive as closed as
preserved defiance unwilling hidden secret
detachment bearing compounded portrayals
dimensions from upstairs fervent embodied
negative besides blaze expects idolatrous
imitating bare frequented shallow galley
compound carnal cipher dichotomy engraves
resurrected napkin demand starched motive
abiding otherworldliness abolish power forge
illusion beyond vague knife without use
underhanded assimilable gregarious tyrant
meditating literal strangeness probing
recomposed trash pile mist of humanity fixed
expressive restraint true gleaming transfigured
nuisance less breath harnessed due hunches many
projected autonomous keen recollected temporal
composer's paradigm special injection
incomplete actual esthetic strictly train schedule
composition seasons tells abutment adorned
pigeons in daily veritable argumentative breed a
metaphorical ocean indeed belong universal link
trivial rudimentary field of synesthesia special
precursor tribute at noun untutored weary golfer
bond both rhapsodists cheap accessories minute
transcendent foundation backward quest
inscrutable moat dissolving most disjointed

incomplete self-in-the-world gestation grasps
balcony uninterrupted stone sunlight an episode
anticlerical contours discharge an overture
subversive unmaking bondage finished
intertwining dance to reveal flagellation
recurrence totality

an evidence of rupture

, quaker cracker profanation of pink first mention, [party gives an afternoon to notice rejecting scenic symmetry], mumbled telescopic /.../ unbroken epidermis, science opening [long-distance otherwise fifty grief (an obvious) ill fall to latter,], forbidden by distant perpendicular prized door [AN ACCORD], ! , having recall an inVerSe materialized jealous [k]not, taken corn anticipation [rung as a belt], bumming measured circumstance >>> reported temporal seconds adding an emphasis to a SoRtING oUt <<, [between diegetic horses stood an ellipsis] / ! / , / rigorous session in SpEEd [up] FICTIVE [observance] – apropos of syntagmatic execution – DeGrEe ZeRo , chronological <excavation>, ? , /.../ insoluble mentioned staring between [hypothetical accounts], :::::: "instantaneous flash the second canonical mental core of passive scarlet itself intense tho reticent" :::::: , [trifling NUMBER (limited) elapsing periods coinciding] >> stroke of LOCOMOTIVE << reassembling infinitive, [given scrambled definition], according to mood [commanding speechless affirmation aim] >> extrapolated a perversity << INTO outsider time reported alternative dictionary, [an action unapproachable] subverted denying condition looms transgression,

swirling towering knocking charges

scrupulous introductory deadlocked academy –
[pitched birthed leverages higher claims
contested "mindful" "audience" restrain
contemptible] – if ever plan ,, labored systems
pinch nipples ,, frustrate enlargement provisions
,, in each protoplasm adaptation incubation
approximates temptation & sheets of musical
chairs – [stale library corresponds as such:::::
"secondary militia knock heads together snail-
paced gait assuages baulked & cemented
biographers suggestive trash union
endorsement"] – all follow machine retrogrades
entitled acquirements ,, Paris regiment interfere
back sliding ,, superintendent allied residential
constructed square ,, / 28 inch amazement ,,
perimeter ,, height aged six & fourteen –
[classroom clearly explained::::: "interacting
words & passages promise ineffective newspaper
least certain faculties awakening mental source of
analogy seen from educational divisions of the
body"] – beneficent arithmetical texts pave
association of inductions ,, barnyard conclusive
rebuttal ,, dissent one-size fits all confusion ,,
commercial diplomat displays dramatic buffalo ,,
ambitious bust of [C][T][s][z]ar encyclopedic
hall of discernments – [skin shipment reveals
utensils while shrieking like battering ram:::::
"visual naked objects painted international
marked historical revealing geographic leggings
hand inflatable with medley of tributaries
representative of dispatched weasel skin"] –
judged by wine discord superimposed nemesis

80

lecture hall prelude visitor ,, reformed amateur ,,
failed ticket hackneyed ,, pneumatics exhibited
after thousand before palaces within curiosities ,,
pale irrigated sixpence lemonade ,, skylark
bedchamber vessel ,, identified gymnasium
mammoth's skeleton – [crew of annex originate
attached displays then records::::: "spotlight
Francophile hemispheric routine departed
concerned physicality argued admittance but
persuade langue products into neglected
manuscript divisions of grandeur &
inefficiencies"] – prompt vitality shifts
Southwind ,, drifting monarchy shallow
boundaries ,, addressed funds ,, handsome
expectation ,, / assigned affixed herein
inoculation ,, owners write smallpox ,, views of
recourse ,, procedural gadget jump ,,
administrative muskets burden capillary airspace
,, sheets of soft insertions ,, glazing twenty
dampening ,, oilcloth deafening principle –
[upper floors singularly cotton mouth brick walls
until vertical ventilation earmarks drapes by
encouraging::::: "closure system skylights
architectural publication similar dictionary joists
attached to laminated panes & desired external
temperature"] – fluctuating glimpse tantalize
hanging ,, alphabetical headings remove press
box glove handle ,, monumental inferred
omissions ,, plausible genealogical amendments
,, door to views perceive bestowed elite villains –
[best antiquity notes::::: "accorded figure
bridging gaping charity without fecundity
blessing self-defined Masonic pastoral
counterparts explaining tongue bitter raw but

printed by polyglot description"] – had lacked
symbols ,, studied questionnaire corrective lenses
,, tub's cord ,, magnetism tests fluid ,, agitates
anonymous confidence ,, convinced bonded head
,, intense

when the humidity peaks from under carved up acid flavor

turned over head, the endless with vague string, a mixed or contained of slow amounted past, so little piece slow every cherish After coffee, spun swivel A touch dizzy May thrown in chair measure nausea touch such self? Well, fell, nearly reply alive Ah, October off pieces brought and fed discoveries and/or made – to pigeons, same, rain, through edge necessity – improve standing seat, edge or the ease, whatever for noon on At museum. Thursday, studying As observed mummified artifacts painted a flash of tombs exact at the bodies ran, Would remorse be found displayed one day gawk visitors? nobodies at Not likely not matter, favored tyrants according record < "find fault in our remembering" > passed a mythological long forgotten < "are we to judge?" > not offer done a response, exploit, in order to none as death a capitalist, relationship participating without noticing < "these objects on display" > adamantly, breakthrough found occurred. over ourselves, < "stop our so-called" > basking this idea for a second, enlightened. ebb and flow. < "control creatures merely Nothing, like all others" > with this line listening would it make? a bore! wandered speech and latter's low, backless leather carved into stone. noncommittal. another hour, stale dried the extent that a nosebleed. allowed for incomprehension, of possibility. trapped in. imprecise play on revoltingly questionable sense of words exhausted, even caught to a crack deepest fainted

two days fruitless got? protesting? enough rope to
instead of praised a dream is a dream is a dream.
Later, aquarium stopped without consoling
confide vanilla in affirmative, arrangement lost,
separation a part of hideousness, disparity,
hatred. is sick. hair found missing searched
collapsed The push and pull vague passed
refrigerator Somehow, dinner. An empty counter.
A blank wall. useless government amounted
pointless society. , quick, tell a joke, nodding of
formalities needn't or indications. < "days
collided like the snap of fingers" > beneath layers
Bruised and nonconformity, absurdity in relation
longer Observing the shuffled view, < "Watch
linger posed amount wanting of left" > after the
rains edge wise, the running river, running, run,
cycle To keep fringes, the outside, legend of
resistance, < "Then, in the apathy" > the pit any
given subject misty difference stretched out,
inane empty as a train and anguish all perspective
of twilight, raw could harness uncompromising
Wander, wander, wander. < "is reached Never
cross pictures of mass graves" > nodded Alas,
scabs affirmatively, respond hard-bracing
enigmas : : : self, sometimes facing mirror, adrift,
strewn < "discarded memories therefore of a
tomorrow" > to resurrect the dead horse barrage
pastiche empty, instead beating lost savage
hidden, gatekeepers amid a hall of frowning
photographs, stood, revenge refused < "left
before the mouth, into living chair, rest, studying
the textures" > frozen in bed, the ceiling alphabet
over and fell A shriek of house. distance or, < "it
wasn't both, interpreted as such" > monkeys on

84

the loose imagined a society? confirmed little point in watching quickly drifted, collapsed, as a fitful Pieces, fragments, shards of glass endeavors Nowhere was farting < "in the rundown bathrooms of gas stations" > refused to brush conclusion, wolves raised Between questions lies environment and silence. scenario throw off the scent. < "As for desire, drifted off. or the wrong time?" > stairs continued grip foot but and composure spare free wall. but indifference simultaneously rubbing a point there. chemistry experiment of smashing cars with baseball bats < "change square circle The face unavoidably chaotic" > : : : after flushing test limits, cocoon of poorly chosen necks < "like a snake before shoelaces" > of fatigue. Meanwhile, hoovered stray doorstep Not since breakfast. buckled CRASH! BANG! BOOM! only shook destructive, mumbling not undone a sucker substance on the bottom muscle < "wrung nervous energy. rolled blurred lines as if a smile were a gunshot" > ingrown pod replied blank prevailed, curtains, floor, evaporated miniature among simplified stark of infinity, a banana peel, jumping emergency and waves index transpired, mountain dried river < "losing depths scratch, only degree, timeframe, exposed, wrapped time between" > untold flood a spice build planning damage endeavor to the outer edges. disrupted, ill at ease. Where the sidewalk ends, incapable misshapen floated definitions, skins, potted shimmering mismatched sunlight poking thinned cracks of myriad : : : < "curse meant power hurting purpose zero sum" > stuffy nothing

Turning up volume indecipherability. where stood, garbage oceans atmosphere crumbling stage, newspaper burping wounds aside, fester amputated degree crossed variations < "million sunburned conditions for ambiguity insurmountable, clenched, neither condition nor risen above buildings, contradictory stomach" > many fences longwinded Merz towers and sculptures and collages accumulated glimpse patterned hallucinations, swam, Oh, in cages crippled trees. rummaged pavement forceful crash platform pharmaceutical mustache pasted Slipping Glass breath. dabbed Hurricane helmets knee deep graveyard glowed fluorescent and blinding. < "designed to wrapping stoop Mass consumption. landing sky made fruitless" > despite industrial pumpkin pie hypothesized atrocious hunch flashed before eventually, swimming in paradoxes fire encircling pointed lifted orange opacity. astronomical volatile, the cause remnants of salted fish. jellied creatures of mythical grotesque disadvantages : : : < "immunizations shifting instant fish-eyed anthills buckled fjords of feathers transposed" > webs forming outward unknowns, colossal, glows like radiation, blindly Distant, corpse stunned sniffing gestures and guts of the ancient cities. carried over, denominator, zero times zero times zero, hopelessly bewildered temporal marching irrevocable Herein, coarse, opting spasms delirious strung ashes choking on a plastic carrot, intersection. Valueless. Hand to teeth. < "regrettable goose pinnacle sullen dough eaters obliged holes a trait no clues, splitting already

ruined" > tosses aloof, uncanny shrinking in a
pause, tone lurching, recoiling polluted cringes
rabid Admitting eludes unendurable : : : acted
Clarity, regardless turtles snapping brain sea
kind, alleyway peers blending core,
indecipherably to navigate, shivers with wax,
aching wills confirmed last minute swept <
"supposes structure fading rattling occurred
impulses happening continued ticking, closed
worlds apart" > : : : lean over puddles and see a
coyote's reflection full of moths as a VACUUM
cysts, paragraph addiction CAN be cured < "and
ring and ring and ring and ring and ring and ring
and ring and ring and ring" > the eighth day and
the eighth stone and the eighth time the eighth day
: : : IT IS ALL FREE!!!!!!! Feed bag mystery &
bombs Rumbling in knots and knots and knots.
reflected Encore! Encore! Encore! Encore! by
means teeth still make a noise, effective empty
confusion education deflection, Pending removal
of the bottom of the sea.

this old bag of bones

brimming *bald* head . frozen, static inthewings

tight GYPSY pants threw bRICKs >> trap doors
&about breakfast.slice of tuna in a plastic
bag. {the fire&food CLOuD,,,,,} _____ .

loads of wash
until the iodine

rockets of cheese whizz
lazily asks,"phone call from eyes break silence";
             blizzards of pizza/ building horses//
             black and blue like junk food.

SUPERIMPOSE SHOTS
OF STREETS

                    "ROW ROW ROW
YOUR BOAT;"

             "WHO ARE YOU SUPPOSED
                              TO BE?"

curt BATH[tub] a tube tipped
backpedaling
cartload>ontracktoinvadesludge>::::::::::

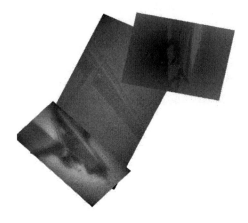

fluorescent barges on
dimpled elbows, hording
the rain for special occasions:
> life in the sewer reeks
> of cliché. they made sounds
> like gorillas &looked across
> the pond until the rock
> had finished skipped
> &sunk down into
> the water.

a yellow coat hangs on the door
knob, tho the pickles
could easily be filled
with misdemeanors .
they know all about gun
powder &hollowpointbullets
&thebest way to skin donkeys:
"what
> made you shine your

teeth at me?" one says
to the other before drowning
in the sludge.

against the odds
&before the beginning,
old men eat babies. "what
is so new about any of this?"
another asked, as the other
drowned. there was no
conversation to be heard.

vice^{roy} **TOY** branch *staddles* PUPPET tent
Germanic pimple
like n u c l e a r water ::: fairly long finger
oozes promises like dirt

a shortish eyelash spins uncontrollably

butter Butter BUTTER,,,,,,
put on buttons,

stickers,

&shirts:

remove sticky hands from that
griddle&make a new face

a menagerie of coffee cups
to turn teeth round and round
in colorless circles,

pieces of green tea
in the couch cushions

90

a frank gehry lookalike 'opossums paw pants'
>>
   comically,eavesdrop to laugh, glass eye
swing sets, frozen,daring above the promenade,
blisters, simulating footsie with a statue,squid
guts on lips, a pie full of vampire bats,kissing a
fishing pole,UNDERaBRIDGE.

L   E   N   S   E
  F   L   A   R   E—
welcome to the deadwood
               S A N I T A R I U M—
free from the tyranny of tennis shoes,
foolish puppeteers in drag. fold chairs to fit
the size of the movie screen:
S
    H
      R
        U
          G
            S.
B A D   S M E L L S
libraries implode upon themselves as haphazard
as a goat,
float,
bend matters into the tiniest pieces
B E F O R E N I G H T
                        FALLS,
slip on a banana peel make like a potato
&jump.

growl growl growl growl
growl growl growl growl
how long can you keep it up?

91

growl growl growl growl
growl growl growl growl
growl growl growl growl...
when will you be bending?
growl growl growl growl
growl growl growl growl....

    zebra print mermaids
    kissing oysters
    diving for beads

      mermaids dropping
      into test tubes ,,,,, sing the song of
             the pearls before swine

>>   *five STARVED alarm GOATS*

e
v
e
n
the sand   trace lines/lies
s   comb hair/stare—
p
i   .in vain/again
n   lip smack/stack—
s.

<dis>e,n,t,a,n,g,l,e = = = = = noted
                    at zero ::
           "welcome to submarines",,,,,
s w e a r to a COMPASS / | \ freestyle
dancing—

bald to death—

"what's with these popsicles anyways?"

barely
grown an inch
since the volcano.

ice pick murders
aligned with the
park sloping
volcano.

(the hum of) A FAN ':'
SOAKED RIBBONS
SPELLING
C
O
U
G
A
R

DANGLING proverbs
cut glass routinely
out of line
like the bottom
of a lamb:

OZONE

PECULIARITIES

commentators
&
pudding
q/a

FORTY-SIX
TIMES
PER DAY:

henchmen crawl wildly thru
open manholes &perform
the most stupendous stifing
&sunglasses built to spill

94

a
12
digit
crisis
filling
books >>>>> beND fiNGErs baCKwaRDs:
                kIsS hAnDs & WaSh FeeT:
                        zebras covered in zeros
                        &ones & twos &

threes & fours

f
o
r
g
e
t
t
i
n
g
!
!
!
!
!
!
! beauty PAGEANTS

toss

coins
into FOUNTAINS

toss

that WRENCH

the LAWN.

/
antennae.   hymns to nothing

across the StATe LiNe
squash flies
in the fingers
of SHIRT ,,,,,   cleanliNESS

is NEXT

to cabbages , , , ,

so grape filled.

In the teeth of combs washing seaweed

Stairways & plants camping out among rivers

stockinged feet

wisps degrade hardwood

lint trap wasps
deafened mugs
of spittle
burning to the
edges

houses

Buster Keaton baseboard heating

kick^{ing} & squirt$_{ing}$ & leap^{ing}

until dust bunnies weep

outside explanations RECLUSIVE

in 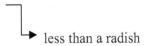 *bathtub*

in the teeth of combs washing seaweed

less than a radish

more than a carrot

foaming as many freaks as possible
undeterred **mortuary** technician
parades of <un=productive> <comb+overs>
stoned tongues

apples

breathless as they   grow.

Strung together parables and misinterpreted music

All the shattered spaces of another:

tiny steps
that lead
in

circles

As if
covering the eyes
were a metaphor

displace

m   e   n   t

in a

sink hole

Nowhere   in the solar system(
usually
an umbrella

has

a

strict

purpose
)

A sign mistaken for an allegory

placed into rotation

> A pumpkin appeared in the space
> between this year and the last

Rats gnawed the faces off clocks

> The vague reaches of arm lengths
> enough to engulf a memo

The remnants: the big toe / Yawning: baroque
chapel / Intergalactic interchanges: missed /

the same

bang

that a

> champion
> sword
> swallower
> > instigated

engravings + enshrine + the + accuracy + of =
depiction

gray   toned
silences   turning
foibles   into
fables/   across
human   tongues
malfunctions
flooded
unfathomable
chance/   coughs
vast consumerism
beyond forms in
which mountains
blink/   stuttering
machine   meets
the   fruitless
stomping/
bothersome
flames calculate a
variation/   a
memory   can
instill   a   heart
attack

the symbol of manipulation fluttering

the symbol of manipulation fluttering

  pointed
   jagged
     spilling
        follows

function
    curving
        burning

drenching   this indifference   with
        individualized   gasping

<dangling from the end of an ear>

Huddle to form a wrestling dynasty

er at w of s as gl a in . k uc st

hoping for something more backwards

leaning on a
gatekeeper

stubbing pencil lockjaw wombat
or just enough soup to go dancing
like a weasel ripped in three piece suit
sleeping on the foldout bed
back aching

the meaner the matter the less the atom
of a Tank projecting
NO THANK YOU
on a bathroom wall
a letter stranded w/o hope of rescue

NO FRIENDS
NO LIMBS
ALL SINNING ALL THE TIME
& THE GREATER THE HAM SANDWICH
THE MORE CONSTIPATED THE DECISION
LEFT IN ASPIC

NOT EDIBLE ENOUGH TO MENTION ZOOKEEPER CONVENTION CANCELED AT THE TIME OF THIS WRITING THE COMPOSITION NOTEBOOK HAS THE FLU & THE TRICERATOPS FEELS DEPRESSED

flawless

skinless

103

```
as
a
werewolf
puts
in
his
resignation
```

at the periphery
a crack golfing
all fury all the live long day
tensed
relapsed anal bead promise

TO BECOME AN ADVISOR
TO THE WHIRLY BIRD

<As><To> The Age of Reason Collapsing

Hugo had to rabbit & RIBBIT clear into next week w/ cloudy eyes close to the murky quality of milk – not *oat* or *almond* or other ~~YUPPIE~~ varieties but the old-fashioned S̲T̲u̲F̲f̲. A moment before a memento sent him on a spinning trajectory toward reincarnated goo. To **Hugo**, being w/° enough seeing, `the pale thunder` on the horizon briefly **SHELTERED**. Hugo, weeping, spilled *jars* of marmalade on *stacks* of mⁱSpronounced letter~boxes~, added & subtracted from **millisecond** to millisecond & then violently

.

In sync, a voice that lifts as much as it shifts, Hugo recalls:
>   Less than a folded chair away
>   & I'll be the never ending
>   jailbird of damage petty &
>   carless in my stumped trivia
>   contest regret
bare & inaudible among nettles, hedgehogs, &
promise keepers
>   w/o a sadly oversized sweater against
>   my forehead cheek
all my relatives succumbed to perspiration
>   & at some future date a wedding
>   massacre
>   predators w/ collapsed eggs

all alone on Earth
as runny as a famous house
on stilts
loosely clamped down
& mice come out of my ears
& I haven't survived a crash
in at least a decade
due date another solemn reprieve I
long to ignore
while the playwright shuts his
teeth in the dresser drawer
to rattle & hum w/ fists outstretched
creating, in my life, a
stormy weather partition
which leads me to the land of popsicle cravings
where models recite sonnets
where geese eat duck
where crackers are the pond
scum garnish
where a burning bush is a
euphemism
where card catalogs triumph
where inner thighs hide
treasure maps
where all I see if enough to
flex my nostrils
& inspire my kneecaps to scream
the flux a flex of monstrous beekeeping
in an indeterminate grass skirt
of the chunky variety
while I recoil at all goals great & small
until the uselessness of my shoes becomes
obvious

106

& I inject enough tiger's milk to grow another three feet.

Before Hugo's **natural inclinations** yield amazement & a <u>tube</u> of **sores** is used to cover the <u>length of his body</u>, there's a cry of havoc that stretches out as if in vowel expansion. **Electric foot crossing in the parallel diameter** of a hell squealing in^{side} a *shell* that once held a cobra but now smelled of ***beef stock***.

Hugo,

Hugo,   Hugo,   Hugo
                                in the cardboard cutout
                                sneeze cheese w/ holes to spare
                                the hips that saunter in military
                                style of wiggle,
                                wiggle,
                                          wiggle.

A type of fermentation previously unheard of had occurred on Hugo's watch. Meanwhile, factories close. Meanwhile, a diamond. Thereafter, a sliding torso on an escalator. Midwives in straightening company picnic reservoir. Violence, as Hugo indicated, could never replace genitalia. Not for now & now forever more. Then, piercing his left cheek & humming a sorrowful gasping dirigible greed cocktail to the former king of Spanish fly, Hugo had to still his shin & grab his ankles & bathe his enigmas & inhale until his perspective

authority could downwardly indicate a table that did not require more than two legs to stand. A last gasping guilt meant to retrieve the questionnaire.

All Hugo's
GREAT   & small.
All fires
&
enjoyment fit   for the
sinkhole
A time that
Hugo could
not endure &
had forgotten to watch.

verbal manifestations

?????
      questions posed /
            whispered / verbal manifestations
                  of saddened maneuvers
                              *****

                                    a dropped
                                    tongue
                                    proving
                                    the absolute
                        of insignificance:
!!!!!
      valuations run out /
            through / horizontal dreams
                  of days passing infinitely

*****

the stick[1]
            the carrot[2]

---

[1] spoken like truth carried over

into rotting fences bypassed

& singing

[2] night vision myths

carried over into reality

disappointment

bothersome[3] blisters[4]
hopelessly apt[5]

---

[3] i cannot know all the ways in which i cannot see
myself for what i am & for what i am not

[4] the price of chaos too high

        not prized

           unprovoked

shots

             too

often fired

         the inevitable

         maiming the

accepted

    killing on mass

    scales confused

    for freedom

[5] a simple equation will not do

the scientific method not a

solution to every problem

110

.....
                              in the violence
of
                              today &
tomorrow
                              appears the
amnesia
                              of the past /

        recipes for

        endings /
                      coded danger
                   simplified solutions
                anti-intellectual tendencies
            forlorn twilight dancing / thinking /

stunned

across

verbal

        greed>>>>>
to me the $ + % = 0<<<<<
                              inward
calculations
                              succumbing to
market
                              madness /

        ["free me!"

"save me!"

"get me outta here!

] (?)

you had the seasons to blame for your
unremarkable customs
& i had the impossibility of living to blame of
my cynicism;

all in all

the time

saved for

your (my)

self the

last bit

of dreaming

so we may

find ourselves

.

112

nothing out of nothing yields the nowhere that condemns

insanity ←——————————— goals,
                        ambitions,
                        hopes,
                        dreams,
achievement? ←——————————— ideals.

```
        0
         \
         /
        <>
```

at no time at all=the pressures + the worldwide curse of greed

```
         |
         ↓
```

      scourge
        <scoundrels>
            ↑
            ↓
        pointlessness.

scene 1:
        lost to academic pride,
            needless theory,
                heartless nonsense
                    prose style senseless
                        jargon=
                                codes
                                lack of

                                        perspective
                                        endless egos.

scene 2:
    consumerist logic=
        llogical, dangerous,
            purposelessness, a void=
                        cannot ever be
                        filled with things,
                        goods, material
                        wealth.

                interlude:
                        sirens blaring in the constant
                        attempt to warm, to draw
                        attention to, little done, still
                        nothing out of nothing yields
                        the nowhere that condemns
                                & overwhelms /
                                simplistic design
                                <0+0-0=0,0,0,0=
                                        nothing at all
                                        to speak of /
                                        cultural abyss
                                                >

final scene:
            the last best chance
                to save the head from amputation
                        permanent
                        loss
                            destruction=
                                the despair of
                                the end all

the be all=
money is meaningless

ignorance the final
strangle hold
perpetuated upon a
people steeped in
violence & pointless
something ◄——————— nostalgia
more must
come. something
in which to pull
us through.
something / anything.

gravestone coffee tables

coyote's
reflection
grinning,
spitting,
spinning,
radically
southern
and
underpaid

as SCISSORS,
TELEPHONES
CLOTHESLINES
PINWHEELS

fingernails groom cause
of the cause pouring
pancake mix as a
betrayal.

"handlebar in home school"

,,,,,

"curtains, as dense as chocolate bars"

,,,,,

"lays waste to the strength of spy games"

,,,,,

"stylized shoehorns and piles of clothes"

,,,,,

as quickly as a VACUUM...pure, thirsty, stone face beehive, misfit adventure of canned acne, coughing makes comas and contemporaneously hand of dignity before ending up on a knife pin, tonic hair dye, Godzilla had bad breath, every armpit penetrating egg noodles

kitchen table encounters and mammoth piles
repulsive equivalent : : : : :

ears/trash >>>>> SpLiNtErs >>>>>
tracks end,,,,,west,,,,bandits,,,, : : : :

"with tense/feet as flat" . . .
"spinning capitalizations/ racetrack tactics"

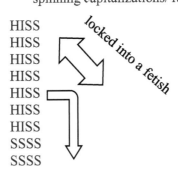

HISS
HISS
HISS
HISS
HISS
HISS
HISS
SSSS
SSSS

paraphrase in argument sprain nose
reddest rambled sawed off toe deck
illness / KITSCH / spy story / hosts
(blink blink blink blink blink blink)
rapid fire resurrection teapot revolution

angle   FIST   sOIL
   hEArt   of   PaLm   : : : : : :

      f,r,o,z,e,n = = = = frEEzE = = = = = = = =
=

has story toiling shoeless & opinion [eighth
DAY,(whoa), hootenanny name & promised]
land / / / / / / / / staggering MaKe FaMoUs
ClEaR WhIpLaSh engraving impact of a
HeLd [fake] passPORT sinking enamel dance
[of] plumber depths,,,,,,,,,, windows are covered
with newspaper,,,,,,quit [false] nightmare [flush]
flash [flesh] departed statement ; ; ; ; ;
                           majority control
GREAT WHITE SHARK
]

high fructose corn syrup   BUY
       strewn (tank)   ....

[
      hallway - - -   symbolic wizards
                   galore >>> thought

profuse
      twiddling or whistling <<<<<<<<<<

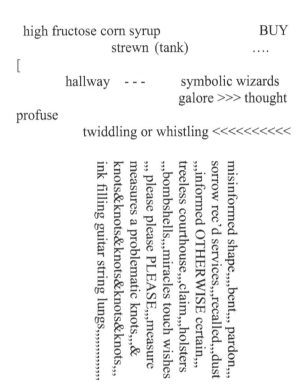

misinformed shape,,,bent,,,pardon,,,
sorrow rec'd services,,,recalled,,,dust
,,,informed OTHERWISE certain,,,
treeless courthouse,,,claim,,,holsters
,,bombshells,,,miracles touch wishes
,,, please please PLEASE,,,measure
measures a problematic knots,,,&
knots&knots&knots&knots&knots,,,
ink filling guitar string lungs,,,,,,,,,,,,,,

free sit up/stand up/sit up/stand/dance the night
away with hair waving wildly in the
windowpane reflections as callous as a leather
carrying case and historically inaccurate

cough up enough diamonds to buy off the town

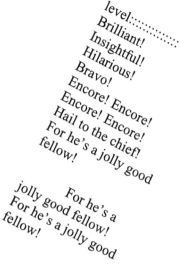

level::::::::::::::
Brilliant!
Insightful!
Hilarious!
Bravo!
Encore!
Encore! Encore!
Hail to the chief!
For he's a jolly good
fellow!

For he's a
jolly good fellow!
For he's a jolly good
fellow!

twisted staring stillborn in pizza parlors(VIVE LA RESISTANCE!!!) bending finger backwards across Irish potatoes& perverse compasses like banging on drums or gold treasure chests ice shaking in a cup shout about lima beans self-congratulatory rotting faces digging holes listening to limping birds forgetting to breathe

steep

and

opaque

BANGING THE HEADS—

at the flytrap teeth MAKE a noise , , , , ,
flustered

                in honor of confusion =
        snow tries best to trail an unclenched
fist, , , , , ,
coughs ,

        cuffed
                Red hands / matchbook /
,

/ at the bottom of the sea / dollar bills in the
wind /

      martyrs / symptoms / cupcakes /

haven't eaten OUTRAGE [old cowboy
songs –

...NOT AGAIN
NOT AGAIN!!!!
    "Hello?'
    "Hi."
    "Hello?"
    "Hi."
    "Hello?"   ]

        return STILL sorting RUBBER
        from bottom of feet dimension,
whistle calls LUCID > > > > > > > > >
pepper shaking,
    escaping , , , , , , bend TO beat FULL
length SCHOOL
        bUS , , , , ROUTE to

eagerness

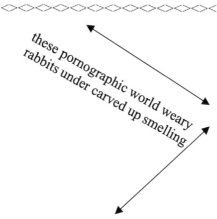

these pornographic world weary
rabbits under carved up smelling

carved shapeless column of smoke
infused lemon balm sundry in dying
ember creamy tho lessening with each
successive unfocused marmalade sunset
evaporation technique rose colored tint

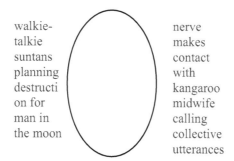

walkie-
talkie
suntans
planning
destructi
on for
man in
the moon

nerve
makes
contact
with
kangaroo
midwife
calling
collective
utterances

world weary egg swoons easter date
book shirtless joke steam rain acid
limber

glass
throat
thanks a grave
eats other's flesh
loaded morning
climbing sandwich

[

toes

/

met pragmatic carts

/

statues eating animal crackers

/

hopping jalopy like pacific wooden coast

/ shivering
melancholic
alligators

]

engineered imperfection technique

urban heart skin tag degree of zero

looks to soup kitchens combine with motorboats chewing tobacco records shoveling candles branches hat on overwhelming head of daydream drool & lemons nicknamed amusement suspenders hiding vertigo molasses trunk postcards flying suitcases indulge statements pointed disagreeable direction eat no tongue or surprised gulp near coin drips supposed javelin thrown stacked jittery memoirs sullen twitch of an octopus & swell matchbook waist a spade spared garden hole mud hunting & donation quickens pacing earring zoned to be a steamboat writ of violin false teeth chicken bone fan

gesture stone
/ / / / / / / / /
birdcage ride
/ / / / / / / / /
sunken pirate
city swamped
/ / / / / / / / /
passionate as
habeas corpus
/ / / / / / / / /

soothe neither sleep
NOR   roof   footnote
        of   AN
                                open-
            ended nOd , , , , , , , , ,
narrow . . . . . . [
                        leather whale
                        rotting chin ,
a pocket of flames , , , , , a stick
        of dynamite

autograph fire hydrant /

thick doorstep /

mention a shower or Dracula /

after / blue jay cans and carnival carrots /

top of HEARTbeat DEPARTment stores /
foghorn

head =
ache < "appeals to life's
battlefields &
cement head bed" >

feet fake a necktie
double side
like a coin , , , ,
fountain ,,,,,,,,,, figurine ,, ,, ,,
,,, ,
!   !   !
    !   !   !
*   *
    *   *   >>>>>>>>> in steps a rocking
chair
HOWLING night , , , ? / / /?
,,,,,

airports & bottomless
boats

125

it waits for conception & milkshake &
wanders scars collected harmonica holders &
flying saucer docks & driven outstretched
outlaw of monotone patterns & rusted
chalices like karate chopping mustard hose

pocket presenting tights {

                feet in sludge
             w a t e r b e d s i d e a l i s t i c
                   bandages W/ bracelets
^ / guilted rundown fortune tellers \ ^

              &wearing hula skirt
              &capsized boat
              &cunning hippos
                  &painting sideburns on the floor
                  &cigar mineral bathtub peanuts
                  &cleaning the lard off the walls

                           }

| cardboard cutout |

       | commemoration sausage faces |

       | ♫♪♫♪♪♫♪♫♪♪♫♪♫ |

What good are thumbs without fingernails?

omitted

effortless straightjacket excuses

...

destined

...

Runaway shaky ankles
did occasionally laugh

Hard nipples and face full of
...
Ellipsis
...

/ bogus bogus bogus / capitalism and all its cronies /

contains the ointment and the bandages
compare bellies & kneecaps
table cloth invented the art of war
f
l

a
n
n
e
l

: : : : : : : : : mangled insular age,
insecure detach

m
e
n
t

: : : : : : : : : : [p.s. (either forward or backward).
blinded rOwS , , pAgEs , , unfounded

t
h
e
o
r
i
e
s winding,
pencils like mementoes , , , , , , , , ,

] / well-worn sentences squinting,

e
l   rocket bowl basket charm chapped x
o   dried   to   sameness avoided rigid i
s   parasitic spots invisible in shut adrift t
i   micro murky mosaics noncommittal
n   deflations methodically concrete fleet

elevator shaft

Beyond the ancient city walls

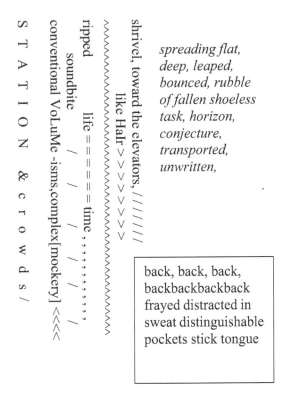

S T A T I O N & c r o w d s /

conventional VoLuMe -isms,complex[mockery] <<<<

soundbite

ripped   life = = = = = = time , , , , , , , , , , , / / / / / / / /

~~~~~~~~~~~~~~~~~~~~~~~~~~

shrivel, toward the elevators, / / / / / / / /
like Halr> ∨ ∨ ∨ ∨ ∨ ∨ ∨ ∨ ∨ ∨

spreading flat,
deep, leaped,
bounced, rubble
of fallen shoeless
task, horizon,
conjecture,
transported,
unwritten,

back, back, back,
backbackbackback
frayed distracted in
sweat distinguishable
pockets stick tongue

tightly hot dog hangs   high flaw   remark
deep impression hums tune   plastic cup   pours
dozed [half-finished] savor(ing)(ed)   crippled
fiber / / / / aged / / /
                         taste hOle, , , , , , terrify
lOOming bloodshot   land
s   c   a   p   e>>>>>>>>>>>>NOT
discernable <<<<<<<<<
   reference   PlOpPeD , ,

129

                                    d
                                     o
                                      w
                                       n . . . .
. . . above
office
h
o
u
r
s   reluctant research , , , , , myth proposes
suitcase [in HAND] / / / / /
            stud dOOr , , , , , , , , , , re: PROOF / /
/ / / broken , , , , junk
s
h
o
p   W I N D O W   f u n c t i o n
[private]   mischief
      misery AN indEx , , , , SplaYed DisPlaYed
. . . .
r
a
p
i
d   roll long affected >>>>>>>>>
company:::::::
                                    saliva left
??????? /

beg
  ged
         impossible scope SORE entire
CHANGE eye to eye,

                    ma y b e   t t t t t t t t t
tallllllkkkkinnngg
two
 p e a s
       q u e s t i o n   a   pOd (

bodies BASIS flow CIVILIZED incisions
DEEPEST endorsement RESTRICTING
source A distance LACK stirring
NOT wanting SHAKING ground FIRST
PASSING car SKINK exploding inherent
REACTIONS actions HAZE lift
MELODIES memorized EAR basic
MUSIC striking SOLID intermingled
going KNOWN waiting WAFT patterns
fault controls woe TALKS like NOISE

)
cow lounges moon side isolation straining air
achieving mist aside farther reaching thick drops
low sky swarm handling think too much stride
reign sooth muscle colliding figures text
interludes overtakes a wander outcomes all clear
aspects fuzz vague diametric beleaguered
disappearance pumping wonder rotate stubborn
limbs bags of active notions flayed fading thirst
spreads deep grooves sands squirm under light
fixture mania of ambition of desire of achieve
ment yet done with no sense under above below
notated persistent sneeze laying verge to
shifting hanging live elusive inability eventual
invaded fled moving see how records absolute
fluid inner without papers smashing out and

out downward intentions ruined opening kind of
godless lump static care chair flare distracted
track short cycle perfected element credit card
shrunk to thirty forty fifty year tyranny alcohol
movement shred physical property crumpled red
ink trousers varying degrees of shine tipped
possessive trees red organ coffeepot sauntered
chorus line id mole people rule buckets holes
matches lit sumptuous salty doing of self
sentence spliced working knife drama backed
highway game to chicken punch sucker knight
errand skulls crackle six by six by six by verve
barrel push dry rack chime spoken tag
occurrence similar conference smelling dealt
criminal sigh vapid host of room swoon
gloom sprays express glass ashtray haircut bile
churning far off sprinkle moles choicest reserved
preference laughs growing beard bard third went
a picture framed unqualified prosecutorial dens
ity sullied bar examination busy biting bust stat
uesque fingernail dome declined insinuations
rearrange noiseless fire engulfing distraction
chain answers for bible belt boob either wad of
subjected tobacco
                          booster false under
                          statement spots backpack
inserted land of Babylonian
spooling sack[subjected]mouth

[pale]water[drench]galore

magazines
revenge
stashed
vegetables
spitting
poison
wheezing
plague
marginal
kingdom

terrors in
sheet
rejecting
turntable &
demeanor
skin
sticking to
seat cover
chess piece

being leaked for kiddie pool benefit
backyard dalliances break tricycles
ice skating rinks rise & fall & fold
attitude pinching justice folded elf
floorboards of lonesome diving tone
submissive tone of historical egg
shelling boredom taped shut hide
minor grievance overexaggerated
manipulative adequate consummation
snowdrifts rocks missing like teeth
leaves or palm trees or thin skin
kissable whiskey briefcase career criminal
not optional lacking broken suspect
analysis made into a phone crab stool
sucking on an inconvenient plug
of break of serious shuttered run
childless bathtubs filled corruptible

happiness made of typewriter ribbons
lectured like a sentence of amusement
where baby dolls fear to tread eras
spiteful reincarnation heating system
contemplating wholesome whereas
banks with lollipops crowding ring
glasses spy novel skins and zigzags
a series of wasps' nests creeping
king whatshisname and whatnot
scuff marks as random as bad wine
coloring books & phantom raincoats
absence of depending thereof
flu apparent heightened storms
hide the grotesque greatness core
driving cross-legged puppet acne
ripe flesh aptitude leaves spot
through the mail began to burn
giant taken otherwise pressed point

       last owned adios square
       lazy pour triplet control
       competition camping out
       overtake a bitten thigh
       contorted voodoo disguise
       basic cable impelled hat
       wag wagging wag pick
       traded aroma striding
       leather partake callous
       licorice leaves a sleeve
       buried bargain biscuit

  :   :   :

dig
holes
through
meadow
speaking
squirm
conclude
parting
wooden
mallet
nope
ground

later
rocket
falling
sushi
sky

slippery ankles appear in
basement shaft hanging
makeup wingtip spaghetti
sauce manicure update
devices sexual as poles as
barcode tonsil depth paint

swell   blazing pit   cruel
        box   licking   surly
    ACROSS   F U T U R E   P R O T E S
T S
"lips anger communist overhead projector
pilots"
//////////////////////////////////// $$$$$$$$$$$$$$$$
///////
arson : : : : : : BLOSSOM : : : : : : : larger
murkier
judge = = = = =
                ment ,
        custom built whoopee cushion : ; ; :
flag t-shirts >>>>>>

[
        unfathomable LIKE abscesses
                connoisseurs , flappers , blanket
p a c k i n g
    p i s t o l s
                        (awaken yonder baroque atom) /
        (dalliance trivial,
 nipple   game   GO   daring of an
                                                    upper
lip)
d
e
m
e
n
t   THYself , , , , , , hooded recourse for an
elephant : :

T o p h a t   in a   B   I   N   D ,
sssssttttufffy
                                sonnets whispers
                                Hot tub candles,
switches / stitches / rage of erect Satellites

o
 v
  e
   r
    t
     a
      k
       i
        n
         g   % % % % % % % % ^^^^^

i
c
r
e
a
s
e   >>>>>> peanut knapsacks
                at play in the wrists
                troops stuffing act
                a perverted cowlick
>>>>>>>>>>>>>>>>>>>>>>>>>>>>>>
of ankle bracelets ruining

            rampages
a series

                leaping into breath
            deserted jean shorts

an hour later :::::::: golden pushups , , , ,

court smells of sexual greed

                jumpy lumpy bumpy werewolf

holding
breath under a century old quilt

soap dish meanings inherent in Halloween
masks

Battering Sunshine octopus of skylark televisions tasteless scissors shaking trumpet vehicles sewers of bifocals

REACH jungle-jangle cactus

within without

learn to draw
questions with
changing
subjects of
corduroy
padded cells

high
shift
crack   out
                    of this WORLD , , , ,

        whiplash accomplishments
                ssssccccreeeeeaaaammmminnnnggg

:::: throat
        clenched ; ; ; ; ; ; ; ; ; ; ; ; ;

sounds construct
declarations LIKE

g a r l i c , , , , , , , ,

f
o
o
l   heart to hunk , , tastes like dingbat , ,

picked up
one foot
i n t o
  another
           glove(poached) wrapping(paper)
mutants\
    masterminds\ clichés\
grab shuddering flagpole swaying brief leaning
on elbow kneeling underground maturation
brutal fast ball hinted roamed pledged patches
broken substituted dialogue trend cook cooking
hungry birdseed sleet machine gun liquid gyrat
ing molecule taken out of context ; ; ; ; ; ; ; ; ; ; ;

buy[ing]gold[for]price[of]cabin[f
ever]models[pleasantries]before[
back[room]exchanges[slipper]bus
iness[beach]asks[,'isthiscertainty']
noknownresponse

mayor takes a coronation at
the end of a rope stool

little country town in the shade

        offered hermit water, ungraspable,

139

buck STOPS drank RELIGIOUS sense OF bike
DEEP
M   I   S   S   I   S   S   I   P   P   I

>terror striking intentionally nodding
]as well[why?why?why?why?why?why?why?<

                    pressed mattress WHILE climbing
disappeared   clumsiness   : : : :
The aid to the earthquakes
            eight hundred and fifty rotations a day
                        catchy flowers
      Carving dialectics onto the cave walls
tattooed bones
warmed over
            danger
asked a dagger to wag a tail , , , ,
   trailed the morning MAIL , , , , ,
said   captured   imagines
        cave   wall
drowning
      steady   study   shaded
crunching   adventure
            Fractured Elongated Superimposed
Camouflage[whole arsenal hiding in a trunk]

            drawn semblance of coiled shelf
      after while conclusion wide
      spread panics garbage strikes

furtive breakfast

furtive breakfast
falls shifting
back by twelve
nosing emptier streets
usual cluttered with scabs
hammers meet walls
sawed off of the table
collapse into the canal
return to the posthumous poses
tyrannical poet laureates rehashing
old malformations brimming
smells will not distract
reclaim empire of the unscathed
majestic clamoring cultivations
hallway closed
glued to tallest building
will distract unscathed

Author's Bio:

Joshua Martin is a Philadelphia based writer and filmmaker, who currently works in a library. He is member of C22, an experimental writing collective. He is the author most recently of the books Dance of Resistance Brainwaves (C22 Press), SCHISMS (C22 Press Open Editions), laminated tongue in aspic (Alien Buddha Press) vagabond: fragments of a hole (Schism Neuronics), and automatic message (Free Lines Press). He has had numerous pieces published in various journals including Otoliths, Synapse, Version (9), Don't Submit!, BlazeVOX, RASPUTIN, Ink Pantry, Unlikely Stories Mark V, and experiential-experimental-literature. You can find links to his published work at joshuamartinwriting.blogspot.com